DEATH KISSED

PHOENIX RISING BOOK TWO

ANNIE ANDERSON

DEATH KISSED
Phoenix Rising Book 2

International Bestselling Author
Annie Anderson
Copyright © 2016 Annie Anderson
Print ISBN: 978-1-960315-21-2

Editing by Barb Shuler & Emily Maynard
Cover Art & Formatting by Tattered Quill Designs

www.annieande.com

This book is dedicated to all those who think they can't go on. You can. I know you can. One more minute, one more step, one more breath. I believe in you.

PROLOGUE

MENA—1965

MY TOUCH IS A DEATH SENTENCE.

Growing up, Mama warned me never to use my power. Never, ever. Because using it could get me killed. "Or worse," she would say, because death is not the worst thing that could happen to a person.

Death is just a step in life.

I roll my mother's harsh but honest words over in my mind as I try to move without being touched through the throng of teenagers hell-bent on getting to the movie theater just behind me. Typically, I would have just crossed the street, but on this night, I figured the crowd was safer. But one little shock, one little slip, and it would all be over.

No more disguise. No more hiding. No more normal life—or normal for me, anyway.

But "normal" was such an inane word. It meant a life of lying, of holding myself back. It meant never feeling another person's touch, never revealing my true self. It meant tamping down everything that I was and everything I could be.

It meant being a shell of a woman, a bitter little outcast holding onto a power I had no hope of containing.

Keeping my power leashed is the real problem. Holding it inside for days and days, as I wait until I can get to a secluded spot in the desert to release the pent-up urge. Like the revving of an engine just before the green light, my body thrums, waiting for the press of the pedal. Waiting until I can release the lightning that courses through my veins—the electricity, the energy— that will one day get me killed.

Since maturity, it's gotten harder and harder to hold it, harder to keep inside. That's all I've been doing. Since birth, I've been *playing* normal, while my twin *lives* a normal life. She's never had to bite her tongue or mask her natural reactions. Never had to watch every single step as if one mistake would tip her hand. She's never had to hide, and that's all I've ever done.

We were born of the same womb but couldn't be

more different. I'm tall, she's short. I'm quiet, she's loud. I think before I speak, she... *doesn't.*

I'm an Aegis. A freak of nature that can kill with a single touch: a species of phoenix nearly wiped from the face of the earth.

She's a seer. A psychic who knows way more than she should. And her knowledge could get our whole family killed.

I shift my thoughts from my twin, who we shunned so many years ago, and try to tamp down my emotions.

The bulbs in the movie theater marquee are shiny and new, advertising a movie I won't get to see. Adolescents giggle and push as they move past me on the sidewalk, and I wonder if there will ever come a time where I could have something like that. The comradery. Hell, I'd take friends of any kind. But the times change so quickly, and the years fly past. Just ten years ago, the girls were wearing poodle skirts and saddle shoes, now they're wearing miniskirts and tall boots. Strange how fast things can turn on a dime.

I hasten my steps while doing my best to appear calm and unaffected. Like I'm not aware someone is watching me and has been for a while now. I've felt eyes on me for days and knew without a shadow of a doubt there has been someone out there lurking.

I've been good, fulfilling my duties as a gentry with

aplomb. Granted, I wasn't a gentry in the first damn place, but I'm pretty sure I don't deserve to be checked up on like a child.

I practically live at the funeral home where I work evenings masquerading as a mortician's apprentice— not even a full-fledged mortician. An *apprentice.* Like I haven't seen more dead bodies than Mr. Hanby ever will in his whole human life. It's not like I have friends, or a lover, or a life. There's too much to risk, and I have too much to hide. Just wake up, go to work, ferry souls to the Otherside, go to bed. Rinse and repeat, on and on forever.

Tugging on the *Peter Pan* collar of my dress, I contemplate what forever might mean for me, and it isn't a pretty sight. Over a century in hiding, and it never gets any easier.

It's still hot here in Phoenix—it doesn't ever get very cool, especially compared to the cold, wet of the Oregon wilderness I used to call home. Every time I think of my city's name, I chuckle a little. A phoenix living in Phoenix. My lips curve into a smile, and I forget the eyes watching me for a moment.

I shouldn't have. I ought to have been paying atten-tion to the alley to my left, but stupid me, I was trying too hard not to shock the kids pushing past.

Hiding in plain sight would only work for so long. I

should have left this life a long time ago, but I so fool-ishly held out hope that, one day, my family would be together again. That one day, my sister would be home, and I wouldn't have to hide who I was from the other half of my soul. That one day, I wouldn't have to hide what I was from my own kind.

I should have remembered that as soon as I made my first squalling wail into this world, I would never get what I wanted. But I forgot for a moment, letting my guard down for a single second. As I passed a darkened alley on a hot Arizona evening, hard, cold hands wrapped around my throat and snapped my neck.

Something that wouldn't kill me, but I'd grow to wish it would.

Because those perfect shiny lights of that brand-new movie theater were the last good things I would see for a very long time.

I

MENA

I don't want to open my eyes. Consciousness and I aren't friends on a good day, but on a bad one? There are things that supersede the word "torture." Every time I wake up, Iva finds a new cruelty, and even though I stopped feeling the pain a long time ago, it's not just the physical pain for her. She likes to break me down, tear at my mind, my soul—hammering the rock to rubble and starting all over again.

I guess I should be proud. I've never broken. Not completely.

Except that once, my mind snidely whispers in a sing-song tone, but I try to ignore it. Losing it just that once was enough to remind me never to break again. But I try not to think about my greatest shame, since dwelling on it is enough to make me lose what's left of my mind.

Keeping sharp is my primary goal right now. Staying alive is a tenuous second.

I press my eyes closed, praying for a reprieve I know will never come.

A moan tears up the ruined column of my throat, the tiniest bit of sound echoing in this broom closet of a cell. Iva moved me here herself just a week ago. To bring me closer and draw the pain out longer and longer until I smashed my head into a stone wall just to catch a break.

If prison taught me anything, it was how easily a skull could be crushed.

Iva. I didn't think it was possible to hate someone as much as I hate her. She was supposed to be our leader. The oldest of us, she was supposed to lead us, teach us. Instead, she is just like any other megalomaniac—she thirsts for more and more power.

Specifically, the power that writhes beneath my skin.

The door to my cell bursts open, but I don't move. I learned a long time ago that reacting is never the best course of action. Instead, I try to relax my muscles into the unforgiving cot someone threw me on. That particular incident happened after I took a little healing nap while my skull pieced itself back together.

I sense two people in my new cell. Even with my eyes closed, I can see the dank, dark stone tomb Iva has me housed in. No windows, no light. Little bigger than a cubbyhole, the rough walls are vastly different from the sterile cinder block ones I've grown so used to. They appear much older than the rest of the house—what little I've seen of it—as though this part was built first and the rest was added on as the decades flew by.

I can imagine the visitor's placement—near the heavy oak and steel door. The people I sense are foreign to me, so Iva must be stepping up her game by bringing in new players.

A rumble of a man's low voice echoes through the room, followed by a pained gasp. Then, a voice I haven't heard in over one hundred years nearly shatters my soul.

"That's Mena. That's my sister."

At her gasping sob, my eyes flash open, and I notice a small blurry hand hesitate before brushing back crusted hair from my cheek. My eyes haven't quite figured out how to focus, still healing from the self-inflicted head injury.

"Mena-girl, can you hear me?" Aurelia asks as she touches my shoulder before yanking it back in surprise.

She doesn't expect me to flinch away from her or scurry in a backward crab walk off the cot, putting my back against the closest wall. But that's what I do even when I tell my mouth to open, and my voice to say hello. Apparently, my body is working independently of my brain on this one.

Especially when, instead of the greeting I mean to say, I start hissing at her. My breaths speed up, and my eyes roll in my head.

Keep it together, Mena. This probably isn't a trick, but even if it is, you have to keep yourself together.

I hear a *thud-thud-thud...* my body moving of its own volition, slamming me into the wall, trying to smash its way through the stone. My body is doing what it used to do in the beginning: flee. And then Aurelia is rushing me. She grips my arms and yanks me away from the wall.

"Stop hurting yourself. Please, Mena-girl. No one is going to harm you," she says soothingly. She cradles me in her warm arms, oblivious to the stink and dirt and dried blood on my skin. She doesn't seem to care that I'm covered in filth and smell like a sewer. She whispers in my ear, soft words I don't really understand, but eventually, my breaths ease and my eyes begin to focus.

My twin knows precisely what torture is like. Iva bragged about ripping the skin from her bones. She told me of every cut she made, every scream she yanked from my sister's lips. Every drop of blood she drew. Other than wielding the blade on me—which is her favorite pastime—telling me of my sister and her mate's torture was a close second.

I know she can feel that terrible ache along with me.

"Mena-girl, I know you're in there, and I know it's hard for you to talk. So you can just listen. Do you remember the yellow flowers we used to pick when we were kids? I can't remember their name, but we would pick them for Mama and put them in that green glass pitcher that sat on the kitchen windowsill. And she would sneeze. Remember?" she asks as she holds me closer, enveloping me into her warm arms.

"She would sneeze the house down since she was allergic to the flowers, but she wouldn't move them because we gave them to her. Remember, little sister?"

That comment seems to be the key to unlocking my lips because I fire back, "You're only fifteen minutes older than me." My voice is awful, hoarse and cracking like I've somehow swallowed glass.

"There she is. You with me, little sister?" Aurelia asks, tilting her head so she can meet my gaze. "It's just you in there, right?"

Most people would shudder at the sight of my twin's pale pupilless eyes, but they are a balm to me. I've dreamt of seeing her for so long, I can't begin to fathom what her actually being here might mean. Her black hair is longer than I remember, the strands wild and loose around her shoulders. Beautiful, bright colors and pictures decorate the skin of her forearms, leading up to her shoulder. "Tattoos," my brain finally supplies, and I wonder when she'll show them to me.

If we have time.

Frowning for a moment, I contemplate her question before I realize she's talking about Iva. I've heard the whispers in the halls. The gentries quiet, fearful whispering of Iva taking over minds, making soldiers into puppets. Bending once-strong phoenixes to her will. I'd hate to inform her that Iva tried—she tried so hard to get into my head.

She couldn't ever manage it, though. That's one victory at least.

"It's just me in here, and my mind is clear. I just can't always control what my body decides to do. No telling when it will choose to go haywire again. I take it this is a rescue?" I say, my voice threaded with hope.

The hope I didn't have the luxury of holding until now.

"Absolutely. How ya doing, Mena?" Rhys asks, his

hand on the pommel of a wicked-looking sword hanging from his belt.

Rhys is the same but different. Same tall stature, same dark hair, same dark eyes, but he's lighter than I remember, happier. A feat I didn't think possible after Iva forced the soul bonding on him and Aurelia. Aurelia had never wanted the mating, never wanted someone chosen for her. Never wanted any of the moors that tied her to our kind—that dictated her path.

So many years ago, I tried to talk my sister out of marrying Lucien, but by that time, our relationship had deteriorated long past amicable. While a good man, Lucien was too weak for my brash and strong-willed sister. He was soft and slightly petty. In fact, his infatuation with Aurelia began out of spite. He was simply not enough for my big sister.

Rhys is enough—more than enough.

"I suppose that depends on your definition of crazy. Where is Iva, and how long have I been here?" I ask, getting right to the point. I know I've been here a long time, just how long, though, is unclear.

My sister's eyes go unfocused for a moment, as if she's using that power that she cursed for so long to answer my question. And when they settle back on me, I know I won't like whatever answer she'll give me.

"She's been neutralized for the time being, and it's...

It's been fifty years," Aurelia whispers, trying to soften the blow but tightening her body, bracing herself. It must be obvious to her that I've been here for a very long time.

Shuddering, I think of the dark—always in the dark. I hated living in the blackness, but so much more, I hated being in the light. The light was when the pain began—when *she* would come to cut me, drain me dry, and try to break into my mind. She would rip away my flesh and smear dirt in the wound. Then one day, the pain stopped.

A body can only feel so much before the mind turns it off. But she would leave me to my silent oblivion—letting the voices of my regret claw at my brain.

The pull of a snarl yanks at my mouth. I have been here far too long—longer than I ever thought possible.

Who did I have to look for me? My sister? My only sibling had been cast out of our family ages ago.

What friends did I have in my old life? I had no one.

No wonder it took so long to find me. *I'd been a ghost already.*

I am simultaneously relieved that Iva is no longer a threat—no more daily visits, no more soul-sucking agony, no more barbed taunts, no more of that cloyingly sweet voice whispering in my ear—and enraged that I've been here for so long.

Seething, I mutter, "I've been stuck in this hellhole for half a century?"

I may be furious, but my rage is nothing compared to the wall of white-hot fury wafting from Aurelia.

Her pale-green eyes blaze to a blinding white, and she turns to Rhys. She goes from me leaning on her to standing so fast, I almost fall on my face as she dumps me back onto the floor.

"Guard her. I'm going to find that bitch and rip her head off with my bare hands. There is no fucking way she didn't know about this," she hisses as she stomps out of the tiny cupboard of a room.

"Who is she talking about?" I ask Rhys, who lingers at my side.

"Nicola," he says through gritted teeth, his fingers tightening into fists, looking like they're aching to tear into someone.

"Stop her! Nicola is the only reason I'm alive!" I yell as I try to pull myself to standing. My legs crumple beneath me almost instantly.

Rhys tries to catch me, but I shudder back. The electricity rises in me before I can stop it. As his fingers make contact with my shoulder, his body goes rigid, my power pulsing through him as if he'd grabbed onto a downed power line. I try to shut down my shield as fast as I can, but I'm not fast enough to prevent damage.

Aurelia's pained scream ricochets through the stone room just beyond my door.

Their bond—the soul bonding Iva bragged so much about—that makes it so if one is injured, they both bleed. It was her big coup, her greatest trick: changing something meant for protection and turning it into a weapon against them both.

Shame steals through me.

"I'm sorry. *I'm sorry, I'm sorry, I'm sorry,*" I mumble as I cover my mouth and nose with my hands. I didn't mean it. It has been a long time since I've shocked someone by accident. Or even on purpose.

Rhys looks a little worse for wear, and his nose is bleeding, but he hasn't lost consciousness, so I didn't shock him too badly. But still.

"You all right, Gorgeous?" he calls to my sister as he recovers from his doubled-over stance and his kind, coffee-colored gaze meets mine. In an instant, under-standing dawns on his face, and then his compassion is gone, flipping like a switch. His expression wipes clean of emotion so quickly, it's easy to see he's trying to keep the pity off his face.

He knows. He knows what happened to me, or at least he has a good idea. It's not too hard to guess what can happen to a woman in captivity when torture is the name of the game. I could give him two guesses, but he'd only need one.

"Yeah. Don't touch the Aegis, spaz," Aurelia shouts back. "I said guard her, not *touch* her."

Ice floods my veins. She shouldn't know that. How does she know what I am? Fear threatens to steal my sanity again, but I force myself to focus. Balling my fingers into fists, I try to center myself on what I can sense. The stone under me, the cool air drifting in from the door, the smell of leather from Rhys' boots, the voices just beyond the room.

"So noted," he mumbles, his gaze never wavering from mine as he crouches near me but not touching.

"Don't tell her," I whisper, thinking if I can just clutch one thing, one tiny shred of dignity in this whole mess, I will feel better.

"Don't tell her what?" he hedges, feigning ignorance.

"Whatever you thought that made that look on your face. That's mine. Don't tell her."

"You realize you're asking me to keep a secret from a psychic, right? From my mate? About her twin? You know how that's going to go," he explains softly, and I feel sorry for the guy. I do, but not enough to let *that* cat out of the bag.

"And what right is it of yours? To decide for me

when and who I share my life with, share what happened to me?" I spit at him.

"I have no rights, nor am I telling you what to do. What I'm saying is, if she asks me what happened, I will tell her. I will tell her my assumptions, my thoughts, and nothing more. It is your decision when and what you tell her, but it is mine as well," he says diplomatically. "Secrets kept us apart for too long. I won't risk losing her again."

It's tough to fault the guy when he uses facts and logic.

It ticks me off.

"It's difficult to be mad at you when you speak rationally," I grouse. "Stop it."

That makes a deep, rumbling laugh spill from the wide, white smile blooming on his face.

"Get your mate, Rhys. You might hate Nicola, but I owe her my life. Keep her intact, will you?"

"I won't ask about the other, but you will explain Nicola to me?" He levels a stare at me.

After all I've suffered, he doesn't scare me. The Aegis rises in me for the first time in a long time. More than that minuscule blip that made his nose bleed. My hands glow an icy pale blue as electricity crackles across the skin of my palms. Heat warms my chest as light hits my eyes. I know from experience that they bleed from a muddy green to a luminescent amber.

"No," I say, my voice lowering to a growl, "I won't."

Rhys raises his hands in surrender with an expression of utter confusion. My anger may seem irrational, but they would never understand what Nicola did for me. Hell, I wouldn't understand if I hadn't lived it. She saved me. Even if she had to hurt me to do it, she still saved me. Even on the days I was begging for death, I *still* had gratitude for Nicola.

She told me this day would come. I just had to stay strong.

I just never expected it would take this long.

"Okay, Mena. No questions. Can I help you up, or do you think you'll shock me again?" he asks in a soft, soothing voice. He sounds like he's trying to charm a venomous snake. He's not far off.

"Let's stay on the safe side. Get my sister. She can help me."

The last thing I want is to hurt anyone, but that's all I seem to be capable of. The lives I have already taken will stain my soul for the rest of eternity.

"Okay, kiddo. Whatever you need," he murmurs. "Hey, Gorgeous?" he calls.

"What?" she yells back, sounding mighty irritated. We hear a large shuffle and a heavy *thud*.

"Stop trying to kill people and get in here!"

Aurelia stalks back into the room, her clothes ruffled, rubbing the knuckles of her right hand and muttering expletives under her breath.

"I wasn't going to kill anyone, just permanently maim them is all." She shrugs and flashes an evil ghost of a smile.

"Why don't you help your sister get out of here instead?" Rhys suggests.

"Stop being logical. It's annoying," Aurelia says, and she crosses the room to press a kiss on his lips. Her quick peck is foiled when he latches onto her hips and keeps her there so he can kiss her better.

"Dear God, now there are two of you," he mutters against her lips.

"Umm... I hate to break up this little lovefest, but I'd like to get the hell out of here sometime in the next century. Is that possible, or are you guys going to make out some more?" I ask, getting a bit of my snark back.

"Sorry, little sister. You're right, though," she says as she reaches down to haul my whole body up like she's cradling a small child. "Let's blow this popsicle stand."

Emerging from that small, stone room is not the balm to my soul I thought it would be. As we move closer to the light, all my body seems to want to do is crawl back to my cell. I've been in captivity too long.

There is too much space, too much light.

My breathing comes too fast. I can't catch my breath. Even as the light dims and my heart races, a single thread of hope steals through me that I won't wake up back in that tiny stone room. That this isn't a dream. That I'm really free.

At least for a little while.

2

ASHER

I'M RUNNING OUT OF TIME.

I think this as I watch my King gripping the handrail as he shakily makes his way down the stairs to the subbasement medical bay. His white knuckles clutch the banister, and I realize he's weaker today than he was yesterday. He's fading fast.

Too fast.

I feel like an asshole for thinking it, but the further John's health deteriorates, the more I know I'm a dead man.

Gods, I'm a selfish prick.

Here I thought I'd get to die in battle or maybe after I got to watch my children and grandchildren grow up.

But that won't happen. I don't get a mate or children. I wasted too much time on my job, and now I get to watch the man I've considered the closest thing I have to a father wither away to nothing. I get to see my life and my future shrivel to a husk and blow away in the wind.

The job I put so much of myself in will kill me as soon as he takes his last breath.

And there's nothing I can do about it. No foe to fight, no sword to clash.

Wraiths are a tricky bunch. So many of our kind are two-faced assholes. Hiding. Scheming. Manipulative.

When you're the gatekeeper to Hell, sometimes the honor system shits the bed a bit.

But the one thing we're completely transparent about is our mate. John is dying because his mate Olivia is—plain and simple. When a wraith mates, it is a life-long commitment, effectively wrapping two souls with the same thread of life. If one goes, so does the other, and Olivia has been sick—so sick her guardians are scrambling to find a cure for what ails her. Scrambling to save her and their hides as well.

The longer it lasts, the more I know they won't find some magical remedy to knock Olivia off the path she's on. When a guardian's charge dies, the guardian must forfeit their life for failing to save them.

That's the oath we take—an oath we pay for in blood.

I've never regretted taking the vow to serve John, never wanted to change the path of my life, never wanted to be anything else once I was cast out of what was left of my family after my parents' shameful turn.

But now as I look death in the face, I wish I'd lived more, done more, seen more.

Regret, thy name is Asher.

John reaches the med bay and pauses before he opens the heavy steel door. He turns to level his chocolate-brown eyes at me and my hulking dipshit of a cousin standing just to my left.

"I need you two to stay sharp in there. Aurelia says her sister is a full-blown Aegis. And from what I gather, she is remarkably and understandably unstable. Do not touch her. If you think she is about to lose it, you leave the room. Do your best to avoid engagement. She has been locked away as Iva's personal punching bag for the last fifty years. You know how much that woman was a fan of torture."

I hold in my shudder at the thought of someone being in that crazy bitch's clutches for fifty years. I don't care if it seems emasculating, that woman scares the shit out of me. I don't care if she's ashes, phoenixes have a way of coming back. Trusting that

Iva is even remotely dead, seems just plain stupid in my book.

"What are they doing here?" Cam growls at our king. "We just got Aurelia's trouble-bringing ass out of our lives, and now she's back? With a sister? Are you kidding me?"

Fucking imbecile.

Cam hasn't always been too bright. As a teenager, he believed all of his parents' hateful rhetoric. Phoenixes are evil. They oppress wraiths. They kill us. And while some of that is true on some levels, phoenixes aren't the only ones who despise what we are, and not all of them do. Every single faction of the Ethereal has their share of members who hate or fear us. As they should. If they fuck up, we're the ones to send them packing straight to Hell when they die.

Cam used to be reasonable, after getting out from under his odious parents. But since their deaths, especially since it was on Iva's orders, hate fills him.

The longer he stews in this horrible malevolence, the more I worry about him turning into a Revenant.

Turning isn't too hard to do. Most wraiths are half out of our minds, anyway. Consuming enough evil to keep us alive can easily taint the soul. Even the most honorable wraith just needs one little push—a paltry little shove—and bloodlust takes over. Clouding our mind, our souls, taking the need to consume evil just that tiny step further, and then we're not just taking in evil souls, we're eating the flesh of the corrupt.

When I shake out of my thoughts, John's silence stretches and grows until his once-brown eyes turn black. His stare seems to shrink my fuckup of a cousin until it's clear by the expression on Cam's face that he feels three feet tall.

"Do we need to have this discussion again?" John's low voice grates in the small space. "We owe her. We owe the *both* of them. A snake was in our midst, and we saw nothing. They took out Javier and Iva. Aurelia's vision saved us all. They defended this house and your King when they could have run. They fought in your stead to save your life. Show them some fucking respect."

It doesn't matter that he is weak. It doesn't matter that his once-dark hair is turning whiter by the day, heralding his death more than any other sign could. He could give Cam a lesson without moving an inch.

"Yes, sir," Cam mutters, eyes downcast. He fakes contrition, but I know he has zero remorse for his hatred. It's evident by the unyielding line of his shoulders and the fixed set of his jaw. He feels nothing but rage.

Fucking moron, I think as I slap him upside the back of his idiot head once John's back is turned.

Cam flinty blue gaze slices to me, but I refuse to back down. One of these days, I won't hold back when I punch him in the face. He nearly signed his own death warrant just two weeks ago. If I hadn't kept him in line, kicked his ass, and practically held his fucking hand the whole damn time, John would have had his head already. Unstable and malignant, I've slept the fewest hours of my life watching out for him.

One of these days, I won't be here to save his ass.

John grunts as he pushes the door open, but I refrain from helping him. I learned very early on—once he started to deteriorate—that letting him do what he could for himself was the only way either of us were going to survive. The room beyond has stark-white walls and gray cement floors, and while it appears pristine, it carries the faint smell of earth and dirt. I suppose being this far underground will taint the air no matter how many air purifiers are running.

Eight hospital-grade beds—four on each side—line the room. Each bay has the required oxygen ports, IV stands, and monitoring devices. Most of the bays have their privacy curtains open, but one in the far-back right is pulled shut.

Carver is still in the med bay and hasn't yet regained

consciousness after a vicious attack from his mate, Javier. At this point, I am not certain it is a bad thing. Javier turned Revenant unbeknownst to us all. A puppet for Iva to infiltrate this house, and now that his mate is dead, I dread the day when we have to tell him what happened. While it doesn't appear as if Carver had any knowledge of Javier's deceit, it is a general rule that most people have a hard time looking at someone who ignored the signs of violence. Mass murder, no matter the cause or reason, usually carries a taint that stains the survivors.

The only other occupied bay has the privacy curtains open, and the rest of the members of the house are loosely surrounding the bed, blocking my view of our newest houseguest.

I still can't believe Aurelia is a twin. I hope they aren't identical, because two of her unpredictable asses would most likely be the worst thing I could think of. The last thing we need in this house is more crazy, yet here we are.

Aidan and Ian block my view, but that doesn't matter. I have no interest in the Psychic Wonder's sister. I just hope her presence is more transitory than it seems. The last thing we need is her to hole up here when everything in our lives is about to change.

And it is. Make no mistake.

If John dies without a plan of succession, we are all fucked.

The brothers move to the side out of John's way, and my King introduces himself to the patient.

"Hello, Mena. My name is John Black. Welcome to my home. I'm happy you are with us, and you made it out of there. You and your family are invited to stay here as long as you need."

Oh, great, just lay down the welcome mat, John.

"Anything you need from us, please just let us know."

Out of the corner of my eye, I see a dark-haired head nod hesitantly. She doesn't make a noise, not a sound, not a whisper. How odd.

Finally, she clears her throat, and then a soft, but hoarse voice speaks. "Th-thank you, sir. Thank you for letting me impose on your generous hospitality. I will not forget this kindness."

That voice.

Something about that voice pulls at me, as if there were steel strings around my soul, and they are finally being reeled home. Without thought, my body moves. I gently push Aidan out of my way so I can get closer. He obliges with a grunt of indignation, but I don't care. He takes forever to move.

Finally.

Finally, I can see her. Her bowed head and downcast eyes are in deference to the king. She's rail thin, the shapeless hospital gown billowing around her like a sail. Her wrists and arms are mottled with purple and green bruises.

And the scars...

Faint pink lines crisscross old white ones up and down both arms. A few of her fingers are irreparably disfigured, especially the pinky finger on her right hand. It is crooked and curled, and even though the rest of her fingers are moving, picking at the nonexistent pills on her blanket, that one lone pinky remains still. Her fingernails are cracked and jagged but clean and scrubbed.

I taste the metallic tinge of blood on my tongue, and I realize my fangs have descended and have sliced my lip. I feel the pinch of my talons growing from the tips of my fingers, and I understand that my body has gone into a full phase without my mind ever asking it to. Rage, the likes I have never felt, washes through me, and I realize I want to murder someone for the first time in my long life. I've killed in my three hundred years of service to the king, but never have I relished the deaths.

But right this second, I want to know who did this

to her. I want to know if it was just Iva or a host of her soldiers. I want to rip the skin and muscle from their bones as they watch. I want to consume them until they are left writhing in the depths of Hell.

My brain seems to split in two. I want to maim and murder, but I also want to comfort her. I can almost taste the bitterness of her distress, how much she must hate people looking at her, talking to her after so many years of captivity. I want to see her eyes. I want to know what she's thinking. I can't take the waiting, and I move Ian out of the way and then West and then Evan, making my way to the left side of her bed.

I hear faint sounds of protests and shouts beyond the harsh buzzing in my ears, but I don't care. I know my hands are taloned, but I can't think about reining in my phase.

I reach out to touch her fidgeting fingers, and in surprise, her head finally rises so I can see her face. Her eyes are wide and fringed in black lashes that make her beautiful olive-green irises pop. Her forehead and the left side of her face are covered in bruises, and her nose is pert and cute, even if it's a little swollen. Her cheekbones are high and sharp, and as soon as I can, I'm making her eat until she bursts.

Those eyes that only a second ago were startled,

swiftly turn from surprised to angry, and in a flash, her irises turn from green to gold. The last thought of consciousness I have before she shocks me stupid is how pretty her eyes are when she's mad.

3

MENA

One second, I'm trying to mind my manners and be as invisible as possible, given the circumstances, and the next, some huge, black-eyed wraith is trying to grab my injured hand. My right hand has been smashed and snapped and crushed so many times over the years. And just for kicks, Iva would rub Morganite dust in my open wounds. Morganite being one of the few things that can permanently scar or injure a phoenix.

She was a peach, that woman.

I still can't move my pinkie finger. I'm pretty sure I never will, and seeing the sharp talons of a fully phased wraith trying to grab my hand... well, sanctuary or not, I'm damn well going to defend myself.

What concerns me the most about this whole situation is that I haven't been in this house for more than an hour and I've already shocked someone. Granted, this time it was on purpose, but I'm genuinely fearful of the next time. It's building under my skin. That itch, that urge.

I haven't felt it in years, but the burn is coming.

"What in the cold depths of hell was that?" I screech as I look over the edge of my hospital bed to peer at the man I just juiced. Everyone seems to have frozen just before things start moving at hyper speed.

Aurelia appears in front of me, looking murderous. Flames are already licking up her arms, and she looks about three seconds from turning the man who tried to touch me to ash.

The dark-haired guard steps in front of the king, seeming ready to tear my head off if necessary. A low, rumbling growl vibrates from his chest. Evan and West look torn between the king and me, while the brothers, Aidan and Ian, are trying to hold in their snickering. They're failing, though, and the shorter one, Ian, can't seem to help doubling over and letting out a roar of laughter.

"Well, that's a crash and burn if I ever saw one." Ian guffaws, while holding onto his sides.

The taller of the two, Aidan, who was trying not to

lose it, tosses his head back and explodes with a booming laugh. That diffuses some of the tension, but Ari is still mad, and the king's large guard is practically grinding his teeth to dust.

"What the fuck, John? I thought Javier was a one-off. Do we need to leave?" Rhys growls from his perch at my left shoulder. He isn't touching me, but his presence here is protective. Like a big brother. It would feel nice if we weren't in the middle of wraith-central with one of the king's guards going all black-eyed on me.

The king appears almost smug as if a plan has come together perfectly. Iva would get that same look when I did something out of character that gave something away.

I don't like that look. It gives me the creeps.

"I believe Mr. Crane's intentions were of a more… 'affectionate' nature than he portrayed." John smiles, faking a cough, clearly masking a chuckle.

"You don't think… *Shit.*" Aurelia pauses. "We'll talk about this later. For right now, can you remove this bumbling oaf until Mena is feeling better?" Aurelia asks, but it doesn't exactly sound like a question. More like a thinly veiled threat wrapped in an ass-kicking promise.

I love my sister.

The flames kissing her skin extinguish into nothing just before she reaches down and slaps the fallen guard upside the head. That rouses him, and a long, pained groan escapes his throat.

"Ooooooowwwwwww," he moans. "What the hell happened?" he slurs from the floor.

"Jesus fucking Christ, Asher. Are you new? Don't touch the Aegis, numb nuts," Aurelia chastises him.

For some reason, this irks me. I don't shock people willy-nilly. Well, except Rhys, but that was an accident. I can accept a hug from someone. Someone can hold my hand. I'm not a bomb about to go off.

Well, that may not be true. But I'm not a leper. *At least that's true.*

"Don't treat me like a child. I can defend myself. I just demonstrated that fact not ten seconds ago. You are not my keeper or my defender. Now, tell him you're sorry for smacking him. That's adding insult to injury; I already knocked him out. Smacking him is just mean," I scold her before turning my body so I can see around the wall my sister is making.

Who knew someone so small could fill so much space?

When I see him, I'm struck dumb. He is no longer black-eyed or taloned. Fangs no longer tear into his lips, but blood still stains them red. His eyes are the blue of a cold winter morning, and though he's still sprawled on the cement floor, it's obvious he's taller than me, and that's a difficult feat to achieve. His light-brown hair is cropped short and is sticking up in all directions due to the nice jolt of electricity I slammed through his system. When I get a better look at the blood staining his upper lip, a barb of shame pierces me.

I don't like that at all. Something about knowing I'm the one who put the blood there, makes me want to cry. The biting sting of tears hits my nose.

"Are you all right?" he rumbles from the floor, his head cocked to the side. He's frowning, a tight pucker of his brow, and the sheer lunacy of this moment makes me smile.

"I should be asking you that. I'm sorry I shocked you, but you looked hostile," I say ruefully as I shrug a shoulder.

"My apologies, Miss. I mean you no harm," he murmurs, and from his expression, I believe him. His words are like a balm, soothing and cool against my skin. It makes the ache disappear for a moment.

"Got a funny way of showing it, Asher," Rhys says from the foot of the bed.

I didn't even notice him move. I scan the med bay, and the room has been mostly cleared. All that remains are Evan, my sister's tiny best friend, the king's dark-haired, angry-looking guard, Rhys, and Aurelia.

The guard makes me nervous, and a shudder of fear

snakes its way up my spine as I shrink back into the bed. His huge, hulking frame stalks toward me, but everyone is looking at Asher and not the pissed-off wraith eyeing me like I'm horse manure on his boot.

But Asher must have noticed the fear on my face before I shrank back, because before the guard can make it to the foot of the bed, Asher is up from the floor and in front of him, snarling. Not just snarling. He is fully phased: eyes the black of a moonless night, long upper and lower fangs descended. His fingers are curled, ready to slash, and the thick talons erupting from his finger-tips put a lion to shame.

The thing that is most worrisome is the swirling black mist that surrounds him. I've never seen anything like it. The rest of the occupants of the room are slowly backing away toward the door—even Aurelia.

When the psychic starts to bail, it's time to leave.

I move my legs toward the floor as quickly as I can, without making a noise. My legs likely won't hold my weight, but with the wraith death match about to go down in front of my hospital bed, I'm going to make a concerted effort to try.

"Stop moving," Asher growls, and I have no idea who he's talking to since he is still looking at the other guard, but the guard hasn't moved an inch since Asher stepped in front of him. I freeze anyway just in case he was talking to me, because the less I can piss off the scary man, the better.

The guard tears his gaze from Asher and stares at me. I'm sure I look like a wobbly baby doe, wide-eyed, and scared, but there isn't much I can do about it now. He gives me a nasty superior look before giving Asher his back and heading toward the door.

I have a feeling I'll be seeing him again soon, and not to exchange pot roast recipes.

Super.

Now I have to worry about more than the obvious psychological issues left over from my captivity. I get to worry about how safe I am. At least in my cell, I knew who was trying to hurt me. Here, not so much.

I am still staring at the door when Asher turns around. His face is back to his usual handsome self again, and the swift way he can phase makes me uneasy. It has been so long since I have phased, I'm not sure I can even do it anymore, but the way he does it is absolutely frightening.

His face turns from enraged to contrite in an instant. He must sense my fear of him, and I wish I could tamp it down, but I can't. I hate that my emotions are so palpable to the people around me.

Asher leans over, his fists to the mattress as he looks me in the eyes.

"I am sorry for this, Mena. I promise you this will not happen again. I'll make sure of it," he murmurs as he reaches his hand out and runs a finger along my ruined pinkie clutched in the rumpled bed sheets. He gently holds my hand, eyeing me warily as he brings it to his lips.

"You will be safe here. I swear it," he whispers against the skin of my hand, sending chills along my arm and down my spine.

The softness of his mouth is in direct contrast to the roughness of the stubble on his chin as he rubs his lips in a gentle whispering kiss against my skin. He carefully places my hand back on the bed and then stalks to the door like a man with a purpose. I don't know if I should be turned on, afraid for my life, or seriously concerned for the king's other guard.

"So this has to be the weirdest day of my life, and I have been in prison for the past fifty years at the hands of a mass-murdering psychopath, so that's saying something. Anyone want to explain what just went on here?" I ask, not taking my eyes off the door.

"Anyone?"

"Bueller?" Evan says as she skips back into the room, her mouth quirked in a tiny half-smile, at odds with the pucker of her brow.

"What?" I ask.

"Eighties movie reference. You missed some good decades. I'll catch you up on pop culture soon enough," Aurelia tells me as she straightens the blanket over my legs and smooths the sheet.

"You still aren't telling me what's going on, which I've got to say, does nothing for my stress level."

"I'm positive me telling you isn't going to help much," she hedges.

"Go ahead and give it a whirl," I prompt. "We'll see what happens."

"Umm... Well." She stalls. "Evan? You wanna take this one? Because I've got nothing."

"Did you ever learn how wraiths mate?" Evan asks me, and my brain decides it has learned enough for one day, since her voice is replaced by a heavy ringing in my ears.

"You know, I think I'm good with my ignorance for a few more days. You can quit talking now," I mutter as my head swims and my vision wobbles. I cannot possibly deal with what any of it might mean for me at this particular juncture of my life.

"So noted. No talking about a possible romantic future with a ridiculously hot dude. Got it," Evan quips. She is a little spitfire, that one.

"You are the least subtle person in the known

universe, you know that?" Aurelia grouses at her best friend, rolling her eyes.

"How about you get some rest, and we can talk about your fun reentry into society tomorrow? I get to teach you five decades of pop culture. It's going to be awesome." Aurelia smiles at me. "Unless you want me to stay with you, because I can. I can hang here if you want. Are you hungry?" she asks, her expression hopeful. "I make a mean grilled cheese sandwich."

"No. I'm good here, and you stuffed me full in Oregon. My stomach can't handle any more food."

I cannot take one more "Are you okay?" or "Do you need anything?" I know she means well, but I've used my voice more today than I have my whole life.

Honestly, I haven't been around this many people in a long time, and I need my space.

Maybe then I'll breathe easier.

4

ASHER

I'M GOING TO RIP HIS FUCKING HEAD OFF. I AM GOING TO TEAR his lily-livered, pansy ass to shreds.

"Oh, Cameron. Come out and play!" I shout through the gym, careful not to yell until after the medical bay door is shut.

I've scared Mena more than I ever planned to. No need to have her witness this. I scan the open-concept workout area. Unless Cam is crouching behind the boxing ring, the place is empty, so I move on and up the stairs.

He's probably hiding from me. As he well should. He knows his actions are disgraceful. Not just that, but I could legally light his ass on fire and watch him burn on the front fucking lawn, and no one could do a thing about it.

Not even John.

As soon as Mena spoke, I knew exactly who she was to me. I've heard the stories of John and Olivia's mating, of how rare it is to find our other half. John once told me that all he heard was her voice and he knew she was his. He felt it like a rope around his heart, pulling him toward her. It didn't matter that she was the daughter of his enemy. Didn't matter that they were strangers.

It doesn't matter to me that Mena isn't a wraith. It's as if someone opened a hatch into my brain and rewired it just for her. My instincts scream at me to protect her —to shield her.

And that's what I need to do. Starting with my idiot cousin.

Attacking a mate is the oldest and most sacred of all our laws—not that wraiths have many. I can only think of three off the top of my head. Rule one—don't harm a mate. Rule two—fulfill your duty. Rule three—respect your King. That's it.

So far, Cam has broken two of the three today, and I'm dying to teach him a lesson. I don't even bother wasting the energy to travel. I walk up the stairs at a slow leisurely pace just waiting for that little fuck to make a move.

After everything I have done for him, after every single time I have saved his ass, he goes and does this? Stalking up the cement stairs leading to the game room, I only briefly pause when I see John in his heavy leather chair, tired and exasperated.

Before I can make it out of the room, though, John calls me back.

"Asher," he says, no inflection, not raising his voice at all, but I feel the censure, anyway.

Even after three hundred years, I still don't know if that ache in my gut from hearing his voice is from the oath or if it's just his innate ability to say so much with so few words. I feel scolded, and he only said my name. John is good at that.

"Sir," I murmur, turning around to face my King.

"Teach him a lesson, but don't kill him. And after you're done, make him clean up. Let him know from me that I am considering his dismissal. Be it temporary or permanent is still up in the air. One more toe out of line and I'll have his head." John's brown eyes hold mine.

I feel less like I am looking at my King and rather like I'm looking at a disappointed father. I hate that, and I'm not even the one in trouble. I'm three hundred and nineteen years old, and I feel more like a fuck-up teenager.

Swallowing before I moderate my tone, I say, "Yes,

sir, I will be sure to convey that message. I most likely will have to wait for him to regain consciousness to deliver it, but it will be done all the same."

I go to leave, and his low voice stops me again.

"She's a good match for you, but I think it will be difficult to win her. She is not built like the rest of them. There is a quiet strength to her. You will likely have to wait for her to come to you," he advises. "Be patient."

"So trying to touch her hand when she is vulnerable and scared was a bad plan. Got it. Any more sage advice to give me before I beat my cousin within an inch of his life?"

"Maybe. These next few weeks are going to get harder for us. You may want to think about that before you go and burn a bridge."

The truth of his words hit me like a punch to the gut. John is dying. Olivia is dying.

And my death is coming, too.

"Aww. Why'd you have to go and pull the death card on me? Fine. I'll talk to Cam first. But if he so much as puts a toe out of line near Mena, I will rip his head off without a second thought. Does that make you feel better?" I concede, but it feels like I'm giving Cam too much leeway again.

Coddling that fucker irritates the ever-loving shit

out of me. He frightened Mena, made her shrink back into herself just when I was getting her to smile. *Dick.*

"Immensely."

Nodding, I make my way out of the room, slowly scaling the stairs to the main level before the feeling of utter loss threatens to pull me under.

John doesn't have much time left.

I know he is not my father, but I have called John family for over three centuries. I've had John for many more years than the people who bore me. Other than Cam, I have no other blood family, but when John and Olivia go, I will truly feel like an orphan—more than I ever did when my parents' necks met with John's blade.

It was merely chance that brought John into my life. In fact, had John not been out riding that day with Olivia and their guardians, I would have died near the hearth of my childhood home with my mother's fingers wrapped around my heart. I hate thinking of my parents that way. I hate remembering my mother's twisted face, blood dripping from the wide-open maw of her mouth.

Looking back, the bad stuff is sometimes all I can remember, even though it shouldn't be. There were good times with them, I was sure, but those memories faded with the passing centuries.

When I reach the landing, I find Aidan and Ian decimating the contents of the refrigerator. They are the brothers I wish Cam and I were—what I wish we could have been. Aidan and Ian have barely been in each other's lives for fifty years and yet they are closer than Cam and I have ever been.

We should have been like brothers, and maybe if we had more time, we could have been. But that's all gone now.

Moving on to the living room, I'm tackled from behind by someone the size of a Sub-Zero refrigerator. Before my face can slam into the hardwood, I smoke out from underneath him and reappear in my original position to watch Cam land in a face-first slide across the living room floor.

"You know, I was going to be nice. I was going to talk it out, be friends, but now you've pissed me off," I say as I plant my boot in his ribs, hurtling his body across the room like a rag doll.

One would think a man Cam's size wouldn't be so easy to toss across a room, but I'm pissed and highly motivated to make sure my lesson sticks. His body takes out an end table and a lamp before landing in a heap on the raised hearth of the stone fireplace, cracking some of the stone with a *hiss*.

Cam rolls to his side, tossing off broken bricks.

"You'd really pick one of them. Over your own kind?" he groans from the broken grate. "After everything they've done to us?"

Cam picks himself up off the stone, his joints creaking, mortar dust stuck in his hair.

"One, I don't get to pick. You know that. Maybe it's chemistry, maybe it's fate. Whatever it is, it's not up to me. Two, I could do a lot worse than a beautiful woman who has endured and survived when so many would not. Three, get the fuck over your hate. You're not doing yourself any favors."

I know it's strange to just be fine with finding my mate, especially in the middle of this turbulent time. I'm less concerned with the fact that I have a mate and more anxious that Cam could have hurt her. Mating is something I have always hoped for.

"Oh, really? And I guess you are just looking out for me, huh?" Cam says as he turns his head to the side and pops his neck.

"No. I'm not looking out for you anymore. I have better things to do than saving your ass from the fire. And trust me, you're right in the middle of the flames."

"You know, you talk too much," Cam mutters as he lunges for me. I smoke to the side, but he knows my tricks after nearly three hundred years of fighting side by side. He travels himself, catching me by the middle and slamming me into a wooden support column.

Despite the fact that the pillar is the size of a tree trunk, I still hear the wood crack.

Now, I'm really pissed off. I spring forward, head-butting him right in his dumb-fuck nose. The sound that accompanies the break is exceptionally satisfying. He starts to retaliate, but he is stunned by the blow to his nose and can't quite catch me before I land a strike to his middle and an uppercut to his jaw.

And that is Cam's biggest problem. For all his posturing, all his confidence, he is just one step slower, one step behind. Then, it goes the way it did only a few weeks ago: the last time he decided he knew more than John. Cam tries to kick my ass, fails, and we completely destroy the living room—fireplace, furniture, and windows included.

Evan is going to kill us. The tiny blonde terror scares the crap out of me.

I think I'll blame Cam.

Once Cam is in a bloody heap on the hardwood floor, I give him John's message.

"You have fucked up one too many times, cousin. John told me to give you a little *warning*. He is considering your dismissal. The permanent kind. The kind where you no longer have a head, and the rest of your body is burned to ashes and given to your family as a reminder of your disgrace. Get your shit together,

Cameron. As the only family you have left, I really don't want your ashes on my mantle," I tell him as I walk to the stairs.

"Yes. You are my only family. Mom and Dad are dead. Burned to ash and God knows what else. Our houses burned to the ground. Our families. And who did that?" Cam gruffly shouts his question, his voice clogged with grief.

I feel the agony of our losses just as much as he does, but I refuse to be hateful because of them. I refuse to be blinded by my grief. I refuse to blame all for the actions of a few. And while I hate that our numbers have dwindled to such a stark number, I will not parcel out my soul to hate a dead enemy.

"Oh, and the king said you have to clean this up. Good luck."

"Fuck you, Ash."

"Love you, too, cousin," I say as I walk out of the room.

5

MENA

THE STONE OF THE FLOOR BITES AGAINST THE BARE SKIN OF MY legs, freezing me to the bone. My body has stopped shivering, and even I know that's a bad thing. The flesh of my left ankle is rubbed raw from the cold steel cuff latched around it. I can almost smell the coppery tang of the blood running down my foot, but it has gone cool now, congealing into a puddle on the stone.

My shoes are gone, and so is anything else that could be used as a weapon or a lock pick.

So cold. And dark. I can't see my parents, but I know they're there. I heard my mother whimpering a few minutes ago, but she hasn't regained consciousness yet. My father has been silent as the grave, and I don't know if he's true dead or *not. I guess all my time as a gentry didn't pay off as well as I'd hoped. Or maybe I've been without food and water so long I have lost what senses I do have.*

So much for all the training my father put me through. He taught me how not to get caught, not what to do once I was. I should have run the first time I felt the eyes on my back. I should have run as far and as fast as I could.

Sorry, Papa.

My parents got here after me. I was alone for a while, and the silence was enough to drive me insane. Just the sound of my mother's breathing eases my nerves, even though I know my nerves should be shot to hell, since I'm stuck in this dank prison cell for God knows what reason.

A man brought them in, one on each shoulder, plopping them down like sacks of grain on the stone floor. It was hard to see his face, the glaring light blinding me long after he left us all alone.

I've been here for days, I think.

There isn't a window in this cell, but I feel the time passing in fits and starts. It has been so long, I think this must be an interrogation tactic. Other than my secret, I'm not sure what else I am supposed to know.

A long groan comes from my father, and I listen to his breathing go from nothing to labored, to panicked.

"Papa?"

"Mena? Baby?"

"Yeah, Papa, Mama is here, too, but she isn't awake yet. I can hear her breathing."

"Do you know why we're here? I didn't see anything coming. I didn't see..." He trails off.

My father's visions aren't always clear, but Aurelia got her seer gene from him. He is the first male seer in over a millennium, a fact he has been able to hide due to his eyes looking perfectly normal, if the palest green I've only seen on one other person—my twin.

It's probably an old wives' tale, but I heard male seers were killed at birth. The longer I'm in this cell, the more I think that the rhetoric and horror stories my parents have told me over the years have been true.

Why else would we be here unless someone found out my family's secrets?

My mother stirs again, whimpering a low, pained moan before gasping an agonized breath. Her chain rattles in a horrible clank before my father calls out to her.

"Rhea, darling, are you all right?"

"Kale? What happened?" my mother groggily asks.

"I don't know. Mena is here with us."

"Mena? Baby? Are you okay?" her voice is shrill now, wide awake.

"I'm fine, Mama. What is this place? I've been here for days, waiting for the two of you to wake up. Did I do something wrong? I was good, I swear it."

I did everything I was supposed to do. Everything. What did I do wrong?

"I know you were, baby. I don't know why we're here. Kale, do you see anything that could help us?" she whispers her question.

"You know I can't see around Mena, darling," he whispers back.

Of course. If you want to keep a seer as weak as my father from his power, you put them in a room with an Aegis. Someone knows. They know about all of us.

My blood turns to ice because I finally understand that I'm going to die in this room. Maybe once, maybe a thousand times, but death is coming.

And now I know what my mother meant.

Death is not the worst thing. The worst thing is waiting to die.

Time passes, my parents quietly discuss ways to escape, with no new plan sounding better than the last discarded one. They don't consult me, but that seems like a good idea.

I'm the reason we're here in the first place. I'm the reason my sister left brokenhearted. The reason she and I drifted apart before she left us altogether. I'm the reason Mama and Papa shunned her and continue to refuse to speak of her.

You can't trust your secrets to someone who isn't capable of keeping them.

There was no way we could trust her to keep our secrets.

As a seer, Iva would be inside her head, inside her memories, practically inside our lives.

Everything had to be kept from Aurelia.

Every day with Aurelia with us was a constant struggle. Don't draw attention. Don't make waves. Don't do this. Only do that. Be nice. Be proper. Do what you're told. I was lauded for being the better sister—the more obedient one, anyway—when I hated every second of it. I hated being alone when I was half of a whole. When shutting my sister out made my soul shrivel and die within me over and over again.

Now, I'll die for real.

My thoughts are interrupted by the ratchet of the lock turning, and that cold, numbness is gone. In its place, I don't feel the hopelessness of impending death.

No, it's the fear of the unknown.

Someone turns on the light, and when the brightness no longer singes my eyes, I realize I knew nothing of the word fear.

A man is standing in front of the closed door. I might find him attractive in other circumstances. He is not overly tall, probably matching my height of five-foot-ten. His hair is long and blond—like the hippies I used to see so much of— tied back from his face with a leather thong. His muscles are thick, and given the soldier's breastplate and combat skirt, it confirms the theory that we are being held by the Primary.

His features are blank for the first few moments, and the full force of my terror slams into me when I notice the leer ghost across his expression as he comes for me. Before he makes it to me, I go numb, and for a while, I am thankful.

Thankful I can't feel it, thankful I can't process it. I always thought that if something like this happened to me, I would fight, I would struggle, I would claw and scream and rail.

But I didn't.

I didn't do any of those things. Because I just couldn't believe this was happening to me. I just couldn't believe...

What I did do was cry.

It isn't until he's finished with me, and what was left of my sanity and innocence lies in ruin on that stone floor, that the real horror begins.

That itch, that urge to release my power can't be contained anymore. When the numbness and shock fade, all I'm left with is disgust and pain and revulsion. I am disgusted with my own skin that smells of the man who robbed me of everything, with the dress that hangs in tatters from my shoulders as I kneel on the stone, with the blood that stains my thighs and the gritty floor.

With my father's screams of vengeance and my mother's sobs of horror.

I can't hold it.

I can't keep it inside.

The power builds in a crescendo, starting from my stomach and radiating out through my limbs like brushfire, igniting everything that lies in its path. My pulse races and a buzzing starts—I think it's my mother's voice. In the back of my mind, I know she is trying to talk me down, trying to soothe away a hurt that will be with me for the rest of my short life.

I can't hear her words, though, and I think even she knows it's too late. I look at my parents as the ice-blue light emanating from my hands illuminates the room. I watch them reach across the space between them so the tips of their fingers touch.

That's the last thing I see as I close my eyes and a scream rips from my throat, power wrenching itself from my skin, sending great arcs of electricity through the room.

When I regain consciousness, I wish my body couldn't withstand the power I hold beneath my flesh.

I wish I were blind. Or dead.

Anything but to see the rubble of that stone room and the ashes of my parents.

Anything but to hear that damned door open again.

Anything but to hear the Primary's disgustingly sweet voice congratulating me on killing them for her.

Anything.

IT FEELS LIKE AN EARTHQUAKE, BUT I KNOW IT'S ONLY ME. JUST like on the horrible morning so many years ago, I have blown up a room.

I thought I had more time, but it's been too long since I had this much power coursing through my veins. Iva used to drain me, keeping me weak and docile, practically sucking the marrow from my bones. I'm just shocked it took so little time to build the energy back.

The hospital bed I was on is decimated, blown apart and melted into pieces, flung like shrapnel. I sit crumpled in the wreckage of what's left of it on the remnants of the floor. The solid handrails that once helped steady me are nothing more than a blob among the rubble.

And the floor...

A two-foot-deep crater bowls the ground where my bed used to be, blowing through the flooring straight into the foundation. The scorched walls are burnt in veins of smoldering black, and the sprinklers that once ran in exposed copper pipes along the ceiling have melted into twisted bows of metal. The curtain that briefly gave me privacy disintegrated to nothing, while the ones in the adjacent bays are on fire, along with the beds they used to surround.

It takes me a minute to remember that I wasn't alone down here. Scanning the far end of the room, I sigh a deep breath of relief that those curtains aren't on fire, even though they are blown back to reveal an unconscious man in the hospital bed. His bed has moved from its position, slammed into the nearby wall, but thankfully upright. My deep breath cuts off into a choking cough from the smoke.

Over the sound of my lungs refusing to work, I hear a *boom-boom-booming* coming from the steel door and a squeal of the metal grating on itself.

They won't be able to open it, not with the metal so distorted.

While burning alive is not an option for me, death by asphyxiation is entirely possible. It's not my favorite way to take a dreamless nap, but I've done it before more times than I can count. I worry more about the immobile wraith lying in the bed at the end of the room.

Fire won't kill me, but it will kill him.

A thick swirl of black smoke denser than the fire wafts in front of me, twisting and writhing before coalescing into the shape of a large man. Asher emerges from the smoke, his eyes frantically searching the room until they land on me.

"Mena," he almost whispers when he sees me. "Are you all right?"

Asher jumps down into the pit of debris eyeing me warily as he goes. I don't blame him. I've been here for one day, and I've already ruined the place, injured someone, and set fire to the house. I am a Murphy's Law trifecta of destruction.

"Don't help me," I choke, pointing to the bed at the back of the room. "Help him. The fire won't kill me. Get him first."

Asher's expression twists at my demand, considering it for a few seconds before he growls under his breath. Stalking to the inert man in the bed, he grabs him before smoking out of the room.

He's not gone for too long, though, before he comes back to me.

"You should have brought a fire extinguisher with you. I melted the sprinklers," I say as I gesture to the copper pipes that now resemble spun taffy.

"I don't think a fire extinguisher is going to cut it, Princess," Asher replies, his lips pulling into a half grin. "Ready to get out of here?"

Asher holds out a hand for me to take, but I ignore his outstretched fingers, trying to stand on my own. My legs refuse to do what they're supposed to and balk at holding my weight. I don't want to touch him if I can help it—not if it means hurting him.

Unfortunately, I need his help because the only way

I'm getting out of this room is with Asher. My hand trembles as it hesitantly reaches for his. I wince right before our skin touches, praying I don't electrocute him.

My body relaxes marginally when I don't accidentally juice him again. He doesn't wait for me to relax any further and leans down to grab me up into his arms. At first, my body is rigid, my limbs as stiff as petrified wood, but for some reason, as soon as I feel his warmth against my skin, my muscles loosen. Even in this smoldering room, his heat calms me, eases an ache in my chest like my own fire would.

My respite is short-lived. As soon as my muscles relax, Asher's smoke surrounds us, enveloping us in an instant, and then it feels as if my insides are trying to come up my throat. The blackness thickens, swirling around us in ribbons of dense vapor. Asher's arms clutch me tighter, and then it feels as though I'm being blown apart. Every molecule of my body feels like it's being ripped and stretched. It takes only a moment, but that moment has thickened to molasses, straining the concept of time. Then the agony stops as suddenly as it started.

When the pain is over, I realize I've wrapped my arms around his neck, my chest pressed to his, my fingers fisted in the fabric of his shirt.

I'm shaking, and I can't seem to stop. For so long,

I've shut out pain and fear from my mind just to survive. It's been ages since I've felt any form of hurt. Since I've felt real fear. So long since my emotions haven't been dialed down to nothing. But they're turned all the way up now, and I can't seem to shut them off.

It has been so long since my brain has been awake and aware while my body just rolled through the motions. Now, my body and mind are one entity, and it can't decide between frightened at the display of my own power and calm now that I'm being held so tightly, so reverently in his arms.

My calm waves goodbye once the shouting starts, and all I'm left with is fear. People surround us, their voices echoing in the open space of the gym. I can't understand what they're saying, but the threat in their tone causes my breaths to speed up.

For a reason I cannot explain, I grab Asher tighter. He feels safer than any place I've ever been, and that feeling only roots deeper in me once his arms clutch me closer to him.

I wish people would just stop shouting.

Asher's chest rumbles against mine, a menacing growl sounds in my ear and the noise dies down almost immediately. I want to ask about the man that was in the room with me, but I can't bear asking anyone else. I don't want Asher to put me down.

And he doesn't. He carries me to a bench and sits down with me in his lap, holding me just as tight as I am him. We are in a large gym, with a boxing ring and weights all around.

"Asher, is the man okay?" I pull my head back just enough to whisper in his ear, without letting him see my face. "I didn't hurt him, did I?"

"I don't know, Princess. I know Carver's alive at least."

Carver. The man I nearly killed has a name, and guilt hits me square in the chest.

"Alive is good. I'm sorry I caused this mess. Umm…" I pause. "Do you think I should apologize to John?"

He draws away, not letting me have that little bit of embarrassed privacy, and studies my face.

"Probably," he rumbles as he rubs his chin and surveys the damage I caused just to the steel door. The metal is bowed into the room like a bubble waiting to burst.

"Do you think you could coach me on how I'm supposed to say sorry for blowing up the house? My people skills haven't been utilized in a little bit, and even then, I'm not sure I knew how to apologize for something like that."

"It's easy, Princess. Just say you didn't mean it. Tell him it was an accident."

"One hell of an accident, huh? I think everyone would be better off if I wasn't here," I say, my voice rough with remorse and the realization that every single person in this house would be safer if I weren't in it.

Hell, this world would be safer if I weren't in it.

"Don't think stuff like that. We'll worry about arrangements later if you decide you don't want to stay here. Now, your sister looks like she's five seconds from ripping my head off. Do you want to talk to her? Because you don't have to talk to anyone if you don't want to. I can take you away from here. I can keep you safe until you heal. Until you fix yourself. Until you get control," he murmurs in my ear as his hand comes up to rest on my exposed cheek.

It's rough and warm, and I feel my muscles ease by degrees, my fingers gradually loosening their vice grip on his shirt. He is offering me a lifeline, a choice, an option other than relying on my sister and her friends— a way to heal without the microscope. And he's doing it discreetly, murmuring in my ear, giving me a tiny bit of privacy back. My eyes prick with tears.

"I don't think I'll ever get control of this," I admit, and that fact shames me to my core. I should have control of such an innate part of me. Captivity or not, torture or not—I should have control of this.

"Don't feel too bad. Your sister blew up a room here

just a few weeks ago. You're not the only one. Granted, it wasn't on the same scale, but she still fried the place."

"What do you mean fried the place?"

"He means I'm an Aegis, just like you," Aurelia says, her eyes narrowed to slits, glaring at Asher.

6

ASHER

AURELIA—LIKE MOST SMALL WOMEN—SCARED THE CRAP OUT
of me. Call me a pussy if you want to, but you have to
watch out for the tiny ones. They are at the perfect
height to grab you by the balls and twist.

Plus, I'd seen her wipe the floor with my King.
Powers or no, John is over a thousand years old, having
succeeded to King almost seven hundred years ago in
the fourteenth century. His succession was not by
lineage, but by the blood he'd spilled, culling the herd of
corrupt wraiths from our numbers. There was infighting
in the wraith community, enough that our presence was
making itself known in the whole of Europe.

Ever hear of the Black Plague?

Yep, that was us.

Millions of humans died, plucked from the breast of life by bloodthirsty Revenants and a King who turned a blind eye to the corruption that was spread and prevalent in his own house. John put a stop to it. Even if he had to kill every male member of the royal family to do it, he ended the scourge and took the throne.

So to see a man who has won battles against impossible odds, reigned for centuries, and commanded his retinue in relative peace get his ass thoroughly and soundly kicked by a five-foot-three slip of a girl, makes me a little wary. I especially hate it when her pallid, jade-green eyes begin to glow. I'm not sure she realizes how often those pale orbs spark, giving away any and all spikes of her emotions.

Like her sister, Mena's eyes glow when she's upset. I find myself wondering what they would do when she was happy. Or aroused. Or if they would burn like embers when she came.

Do not pop a boner when she's on your lap, moron.

It takes me a while to collect myself, only aware of the conversation in the periphery of my consciousness. Mena's thin body is still in my arms, and even after all the drama of this ridiculously long day, even though she is so painfully thin and injured, I still want her. I see past her wounds, her apparent malnourishment, her scars, her fear, to see the beautiful, strong woman she is. My dick obviously doesn't give a shit about any of it.

Well, at least the two brains are on the same page.

"Granted, Mena's power makes mine look like a rowboat next to an aircraft carrier, but I have the ability all the same." Aurelia's voice breaks through my thoughts, and she crosses her arms over her chest in a threatening manner, glaring at me.

"Was this a secret?" I ask, genuinely confused.

"No, I just hadn't had the chance to go through the laundry list of familial dramas with my sister, and I would have preferred to tell her my shit myself," she says with an exasperated huff, tossing her hands up.

Aurelia turns her body slightly toward her sister, effectively dismissing me, even though Mena's fingers are wrapped around the fabric at my neck.

I look over Mena's shoulder and meet John's eyes. He is weary and doesn't seem even a little bit surprised. He does, however, look worse in just the few hours since I last saw him. I think he has been ducking Cameron and me—not that it's that hard to duck Cam—to go see Olivia. His brow furrows in distress and exhaustion, his shoulders droop.

I shouldn't let Mena get this close to me, shouldn't let this beautiful, fragile woman rely on me when I'll be leaving her. Looking at John again, my fingers ache to hold Mena closer—to clutch her to me until I'm ripped away from her. My chest feels like someone has torn out my heart.

I won't get to see her happy or well.

I won't get to do anything but leave her.

She's gone through enough. I can't put her through more. Why would John encourage me to pursue Mena if I was just going to die before I could keep her? No one is that cruel.

Bringing my hand to the back of Mena's neck as she calmly talks to her sister, I shift her body closer to mine and brush my lips against her temple before pulling back. Her words stall out for a moment, and she turns her glowing amber eyes to me.

"What was that for?" she murmurs.

"It's time for me to go, Princess. Are you good with Half-Pint over here or do you want me to make other plans?" I ask her, only half-hoping she picks door number two and kicking myself for it. I can't in good conscience let her rely on me. Not when I'll just fail her.

"I think I'm okay for right now, but I do want to know about the man—*err*—Carver. Could you find out if he's all right?" she asks sheepishly as she ducks her head, a blush spreading up her neck to her cheeks.

"Sure thing, Princess," I say as my hand reaches

down to her hips to shift her off me to the bench, and I freeze.

There at her hip is a significant bump, the bone of her femur jutting out of the socket.

"Jesus Christ, Mena. Your hip is dislocated," I rasp in horror. How long has she been like this that she isn't screaming the house down in pain?

"What?"

"Didn't you notice when you walked? *Can* you walk?" I ask in disbelief. How could she endure so much pain and not notice?

She pauses, and then her eyes go wider as she whispers, "I-I don't think I've walked in weeks, Asher."

Well, fuck that.

"Ian!" I bellow, my gaze searching the open expanse of the gym for the one person I know who has the most medical knowledge in this ragtag bunch.

"You rang? I was busy making sure the oxygen was shut off in the med bay. No one needs the house to go boom," he says as he jogs up from my left, already holding his med duffle. I guess after the commotion he was ready for action—and amen for the backup med supplies in the locker room.

"I think her hip is dislocated," I tell him, gently clutching her to me as if she were spun glass. Her body is vibrating with distress, and it kills me to have her so fearful.

Uncharacteristically silent, Ian's eyebrows rise halfway up his forehead in surprise.

"I want to know why no one checked her before now," I demand. "I want to know how this got past everyone. I know she's a phoenix, and they heal from damn near everything, but fuck, man."

Mena sits there on my lap in shock. Her expression of utter confusion would be cute if it didn't piss me off that she's been injured this whole fucking time while we did nothing.

"She didn't say anything, Asher. We were waiting for the morning so she could get used to us before doing a med check," Aurelia murmurs, her tone contrite.

I want to yell at her, but seeing how shaky Mena is, I understand her logic. There is almost nothing that can kill a phoenix true dead, their healing rates remarkable. Unless a wound came into contact with Morganite, a phoenix could heal from a cut in minutes, broken bones in hours—hell, I heard Rhys healed from a decapitation in less than a week.

Aurelia must have assumed if she needed assistance, she would have asked for it, not realizing Mena had been in captivity so long she wouldn't know to ask for help. And I didn't know if Mena would have allowed someone to prod her at all—even if it was her sister doing the prodding.

Ian moves to touch Mena, and she wakes up enough from her dazed stupor to flinch back. She burrows into me, ripping a snarl from my throat before I can think about what I'm doing. I want to comfort Mena, reassure her—tell her it will be fine, that she has nothing to worry about—but I can't get past my dueling emotions to open my mouth to soothe her.

Aurelia shoulders Ian out of the way, and she roughly grabs Mena's face in her hands. I don't like that, but I rein in my growling objection by the skin of my teeth.

"Ian is a good man. He is not going to harm you. He has been to battle with me, fought with me, nearly died with me, and I would risk my life to protect his. You can trust him. I swear it," Aurelia tells her, giving Ian probably the best compliment a wraith can get.

A wraith's honor is determined by how many would fight alongside him. Telling Mena this is probably a better apology than anything she could offer to John. Mena nods as she shudders out a breath, looking at me for a moment before nodding at Ian to proceed. Then I have to brace myself, so I don't rip his arms off as he pokes and prods her to assess her injury.

"You have to tell me if it hurts, Mena," Ian instructs her.

She's clenching her teeth, but it looks like she's straining, not in pain.

"How are you just sitting there?" Ian asks, seeming baffled.

"It doesn't hurt, I'm just t-trying not to shock you."

"Mena, you should be screaming," Ian tells her while Aurelia nods just behind him. Her eyes are wide and worried, her face looking mildly green.

"I don't feel pain anymore," Mena tells him. "I haven't for years."

"So I don't need to dope you up on pain meds before I pop this back in? By the look on Asher's face, if I don't treat you like crystal, he's going to rip my head off."

Ian steps back, leveling me with his physician stare, and I remember that he's seen more than we all give him credit for. Ian isn't a child, and despite his youth and genial nature, Ian would knock me out before he'd let me keep him from helping someone in need.

"I think it would be better if you stepped out for this," he says to me before turning to Aurelia. "You too, Squirt. Beat it. You look like you're about to puke."

"Dislocated joints make me want to hurl, so sue me," she bites back irritably as she turns and walks toward Rhys, who's sitting on the concrete steps leading up to the main house. She curls herself like a cat and sits on his lap, hiding her face in his shoulder as he gently rubs her back. I guess she's staying.

"Why do I have to leave?" I ask, logically knowing the answer, but unable to let that rule my mind. The ruling force in my brain says to stay—to protect—and no amount of logic is going to override it. Pulling me from my woman? I don't think so.

"Because I like my head firmly attached to my body," he says, like any teenager would say "Duh," and I'm reminded once again how young Ian is.

Sure, he may be just over a century old, but he's still the youngest person in the room.

John's grave voice sounds behind Ian, and his tone brooks zero argument. "Your mate has to have another man's hands on her and is most likely going to be in pain. You need to leave this room so she can get the treatment she needs." I wince at John's tone as Mena stiffens. I instantly feel like an asshole for holding Ian up. I don't realize the implications of what John said until Mena sucks in a breath.

"Mate?" Mena breathes in my ear.

Oh, shit.

Glaring at John for a beat, I stand with Mena in my arms and gently set her on the bench.

"We'll talk about it later, Princess," I whisper in her ear before straightening.

"Oh, sure. In between me blowing up rooms and shocking the ever-living fuck out of people, we'll just pencil it in," she snaps, and the quip is laced with enough sarcasm that it startles a laugh out of me.

"Soon. We'll talk about it soon. Yeah?" I say, even though I have zero plans to do so.

How could I possibly explain the mating? That I couldn't seal that bond no matter how much my body, my mind, screamed at me to do so?

Because I had a death sentence looming over me, and no amount of love, or fate, or optimism was going to change that.

And I couldn't pull her down with me.

Searching Mena's eyes, I'm speared with the bitterness of all the things I'll never have. I'll never have her any closer than she is right now, never get to merge our souls into one.

Mena raises an eyebrow at me, suspicion all over her expression before her face falls already wiping it clean of emotion so quickly I almost miss it.

She'll never really be mine, I remind myself.

And that's for the best.

7

MENA

HE'S NOT GOING TO EXPLAIN A FREAKING THING TO ME, I THINK as Asher's mouth settles into a firm line. His eyes appear half-pissed and half-sad. Like he's struggling with something but has forbidden himself from saying anything.

I haven't spent that much time with Asher, but already I can tell getting words out of him will take some engine grease and quite possibly a crowbar. Honestly, I'd rather skip the part where he has to let me down slow.

"Okay. We'll talk about it later," I concede with a shrug, shaking my head.

In the grand scheme of things, I have a pretty good

idea of what he'll say. I mean, honestly? Who would pick a girl like me? I'm not sure how this whole wraith mating stuff goes, but if the man has a choice, he has to prefer a better crop than me.

So what if I felt a connection to the first man probably ever? So what if I clung to him like a monkey on a tree? So what if I feel safe with him, a feeling I haven't had in a very long time? So. What.

I don't deserve a man like him. After the lives I've taken... happiness just isn't in the cards for me.

"I'm fine. It's not going to hurt. I didn't even notice it was dislocated before now. It'll get popped back in, I'll be able to heal and walk. Win-win. You can go," I tell him, my voice sounding almost dead, even to my own ears.

I need to cut this off as soon as possible. His expression is reluctant, but he needs to go.

"Come on, Asher," Evan says at his elbow, as she escorts him from the room, practically dragging him behind her up the stairs.

My eyes linger on the steps long after he disappears behind the door at the top, and in those moments, I take the time to shore up my heart. I don't need to rely on Asher. I shouldn't even lean on Aurelia or Rhys or prey on the hospitality of the wraiths.

I should do the right thing. For once, I should do what I've always needed to.

But I need to be able to walk to do it.

Taking a deep breath, I shift my gaze to Ian, who is patiently waiting for me to get my shit together enough to let him do his job.

"Thank you for helping me. I'll do my very best to rein in my ability. If you feel uncomfortable putting your hands on me, I understand," I say, my words burning me as they haltingly tumble from my mouth.

"Meh." He shrugs. "You haven't killed anyone yet. I'll risk it."

That flippant comment is like an open-handed slap in the face, so sharp I have to close my eyes to the sting. It takes everything I have in me not to cry, but a hole splits wide open in my chest all the same. The blistering ache of regret settles in my belly, and I have to grit my teeth against the burn.

When I open my eyes again, Ian's dark-brown gaze is knowingly compassionate.

"If I could teach you to do it yourself, I would, but this can't be done alone," he whispers, "You'll just have to try your best, okay?"

Nodding, I brace myself more against my abilities than the pain. I center myself, concentrating on Ian's kindness, his happiness. I focus on his light, refusing to let the blight that is my powers affect him.

Gently, he places his right hand on the inside of my knee, his left on the outside of my thigh. He locks eyes with me and inclines his head. Taking a deep breath, I nod for him to continue, and he wrenches my leg, pulling it to him first before letting it go.

The joint makes a horrible squelching noise before I hear a huge *pop* and the bone settles back into place.

And then I promptly empty the contents of my stomach on Ian's boots.

"Well, that hurt," I rasp before passing out right there on the bench.

"You simply cannot rely on your abilities, Mena. What if you are drained or injured? You have to learn how to defend yourself, darling girl," Papa urges, tossing me the blade. I awkwardly catch it, fumbling a little before nearly slipping in the forest bracken beneath my slick shoes. I look at my father's face—Aurelia and I inherited our sharp cheekbones from our father. Aurelia also got the paleness of her eyes from him.

My poor sister. Sometimes I just wish I could hug her. She is so alone in this family.

"Is there some reason I need to train for combat—which is ridiculous in its own right—wearing this silly corset?" I ask, irritated, sorrowful, and marginally confused.

My mother just started making Aurelia and I wear them. She said they were what all respectable young ladies wore, and now that we were becoming women, we needed to dress appropriately. I hate them. They are tight and uncomfortable and completely unnecessary.

"I am only twelve, can't I be a child a bit longer before the world falls on my head?" *I only talk this way when no one is around. If my mother or Aurelia heard me be this bold, I would never hear the end of it.*

"No. You cannot." Papa's voice rises nearly to a shout.

Appropriately chastened, I duck my head. He's right, my father. I cannot wait for a better time, can't relegate myself to the wishes of a whimsical child.

My abilities have always been evident, even as a baby, just as Aurelia's have, but now that our monthlies have started, we are infinitely more potent. This frightens my parents, I think—to have two children so powerful. To trust this big of a secret to a child.

I don't tell them that it frightens me as well. That I fear myself.

Fear what I'm capable of.

Fear what I've yet to learn.

Fear what the future holds.

I need to stop whining and focus on the lesson my father is trying to teach me.

"I am sorry, Papa. I know you are trying to protect me. I shall focus," I tell him, my eyes downcast.

"Good. You know, you sounded like your sister just then," he says, amused, and it startles me enough to snap my gaze back to him. He seems proud of Aurelia, and I think I love my father just a bit more for that. He so rarely speaks of her to me.

"All right, Papa. Show me how to use this infernal thing," I order in my haughtiest tone.

Giving him a bit of my twin since she can't be here to do it.

I wake up nestled in the softness of a down comforter, the covers pulled up to my chin, remembering that one happy memory of my father.

Before the training started in earnest.

Before Aurelia was shunned.

Before I killed him.

I wish I had known. I'm pretty sure I would have left

back then, saved them from the cancer that is my very existence.

A faint sizzle and crack of a fire hisses in the periphery of my consciousness, and I become aware of my body for the first time in a long time and immediately regret it, wishing I could go back to the painless state I was in before.

My first thought is how hungry I am, followed directly by an ache in my joints so fierce my appetite dies a quick and bloody death. A soft rap on the door pulls my focus from my bones to the blonde oak door. The doorknob turns, and Aurelia's head pops around it to check on me. Her expression wary, she shoulders the door open, holding a tray laden with every bland breakfast food imaginable. There is toast and scrambled eggs and small golden-brown cubes of potatoes.

"I figured you'd be hungry, and I brought some over-the-counter painkillers to help with the remnants of the pain," she says. "We had Ian check you over while you were passed out. He didn't find anything else during his exam, and you should be healed up in a few more hours."

Her voice sounds like she's saying she's sorry, but I have no idea what she has to apologize for. As always with my twin, I never have to wait to know what's on her mind. She sets the tray down on a wide mahogany nightstand. She sits next to me in the crook of my hip, handing me two white pills and a glass of water. Gleefully, I pop them into my mouth, taking a swig of water to wash them down.

"I'm sorry I left you to deal with that by yourself. I know it can't be easy being here, and it's my responsibility to make you safe. I didn't see you before. I-I should have seen you in that hell. I should have go-gotten you out," she says, her voice clogged with tears and guilt, the sound giving me a strange ache deep in my chest.

"Why would it have been your responsibility? You didn't shove me in that cell. As far as I can tell, all you've ever wanted from me is to be a sister to you. I'm the one who failed you. More than you know. I have done things... Things that I wish I could take back," I end on a whisper.

Well, isn't that the understatement of the century?

I bite my tongue to avoid blurting out my sins. As hard as our parents were, as much as she went through with all of us, I still have no doubt she would hate me forever for what I've done.

Aurelia grabs my ruined left hand, giving it a gentle squeeze. "I think we've all done things we're not proud of. We've all done things we wish we could take back. My sins are no different from yours. No matter what you think you've done, no matter what sins you think you have on your soul, I'll still love you."

All I can do is nod. Sure, she says that now, but I can't know how she'll react when I tell her. I can't know... And I can't lose her before I'm ready.

I need these last few days.

Studying her face, I memorize what is already burned into my brain. The shape of her eyes, the slope of her nose, the sharp cut of her cheekbones. My eyes drift to the colorful swirls on her arms. The artist who created them makes me almost weep at their beauty. I look closer and notice slight ridges hidden underneath the pictures.

Scars.

"Your tattoos are beautiful," I say as I reach out to touch her arm. It is a testament to how much she trusts me that she doesn't flinch when my fingers make contact. I haven't seen ink like this. As a phoenix, I am no stranger to tribal markings—most of our males have them in some form or another—but these are something else. Realistic pictures mixed with brilliant splashes of color cover every available millimeter of skin from her wrist to the crown of her shoulder.

"Thank you. I drew most of them. My friend Max inked them."

"Do you think I should get my scars covered?" I ask, but I'm not sure I care either way.

I haven't inspected my body in ages, not after the first few scars. I was vain before my incarceration. I knew I was beautiful, and it was a solace to me when my life changed from simply lonely to completely solitary.

Well, I'm not vain now. I haven't seen a mirror in half a century, and I'm not sure I want to. Looking down at the exposed skin of my arms, I run a single finger over the crosshatched raised flesh. My abdomen and legs are worse. There isn't enough ink in the world to cover this much skin.

"I think you should do what feels right. I covered my scars because I needed to, but ink may not be the right answer for you. You'll have to decide for yourself," she tells me, drawing my gaze from my ruined skin to her face.

"When did you get so smart?"

A ghost of a smile crosses her lips. "Fairly recently, if you can believe it. Rhys helped me get my shit together. I wasn't doing so well for a while there. Now that Iva is out of the picture and my Aegis finally came back, I'm doing much better."

"Did you lose it?"

"My Aegis? Yeah. Iva did something to me—

suppressing it or draining me—I'm not sure which, and I was in real pain for a while. I was beginning to see why Oracles cut their eyes out, if you catch my drift. When she died, it started coming back. Now, I'm as strong as I was before."

I knew the feeling, only Aurelia's Aegis helped her. Mine didn't do the same for me.

"That's what I'm worried about," I whisper, dropping my gaze.

"We'll figure it out. You're not alone anymore," she says as she reaches for the tray piled with food, placing it on my lap.

"Now eat until you can't fit in another bite. I actually cooked, so be happy. It's a rare occurrence."

I choose a piece of toast, tearing off a corner and popping it into my mouth, relishing the buttery goodness.

"Well, the toast passes inspection," I say around a mouthful of food.

"Good. Eat up, and then you can have a nice Epsom salt bath. It'll help loosen your muscles and ease your joints. Then we get to try walking. It'll be a hoot," she says with a smile and cute scrunch of her nose.

I can't be the cold one anymore, can't be stoic or aloof when this great surge of gratitude steals through me. Lurching forward, I give her a hug hard enough to startle an "Oof" out of her.

"Love you," I murmur.

"Love you back."

I squeeze her for a second before pulling back and stuffing my face, earning me a brilliant smile.

I'm going to miss her so much, I think, vowing to soak in all of this goodness. It will need to tide me over when it's all gone.

When I'm gone.

8

ASHER

I'm losing it.

I'm losing everything, and as much as I claw and scrape and grab, time is slipping through my fingers. John is fading away.

Mena.

She is the one thing I never had ahold of. The one thing I wanted most. But she isn't a thing. She isn't a toy I can't play with, some inanimate object I just can't grasp. She is a person, a woman, probably the strongest person I have ever met. And the one person I will never, ever have.

As soon as Evan dragged me from the gym, I went to

my quarters and systematically destroyed every break-able object I could get my hands on. Lamps, tables, mirrors... I even ripped apart the books and smashed my favorite reading chair. I needed to release all my help-less anger, my righteous indignation at the unfairness of this whole mess. I couldn't protect her. I couldn't take her pain away. I couldn't rip her tormentor to shreds. I couldn't do anything.

I need to let her go.

But as much as I have to release her from my heart and mind, my selfish heart refuses to let her go. I gave up on my destruction, and went to the king's chambers, looking for a reason to not crawl in a hole and die, maybe. Looking for a reason to matter. Looking for anything that will keep me from staring death in the face.

I caught John trying to travel—the smoke swirling around him in great churning arcs, but never taking him anywhere. A piece of my heart withered at that moment, and I had to grit my teeth against the burn.

In the beginning, traveling is difficult—almost unbearable for a young one to achieve. It takes so much out of us, but the pain eventually goes away. At the end of our lives... it becomes impossible.

John is at the end.

I knew where he wanted to go, so against my better judgment, I called Cam—who now seems to have a permanent crook to his nose—and we took him to Olivia.

And here we sit, Cam and I, perched on dainty chintz chairs in the sitting room outside the royal suite. Cam looks ravaged, pain stark on his face, and I realize —like me—he is losing a father figure, a mentor, a friend. It's so easy for me to discount Cam, to take the fact that he's a flaming asshole most of the time for granted.

But he's losing his life—just like me.

Unable to take the silence anymore, I gingerly rise from the fragile chair and stalk to the sideboard to partake of the bourbon stash. I'm even nice and pour Cam a healthy measure, handing him the glass without a word. His expression is almost grateful as he accepts the tumbler, but he doesn't sip the amber liquid. Gently, he rolls the glass in his hands, staring into the mouth of the tumbler as if it holds the secrets we've all been searching for.

Studying the silent man for a moment, I realize I missed something big. I wouldn't have known anything were amiss if I hadn't witnessed the drip of tears falling from his chin.

"Cam?"

I've never seen my cousin cry. Not when he broke his arm in three places as a child, not when he had to put his favorite dog to sleep, not after he came back to us covered in soot, informing the king that his parents were dead. Not ever.

Cam opens his mouth to speak and then shuts it again. He takes a swig of the bourbon as if it will give him the courage.

"I don't know if you ever realized this, but my mother was a horrible woman," he begins, his voice sounding like it has been run over broken glass. I'm so shocked that he's talking about his mother that I can't say another word. Cam has always hated talking about his parents.

Struck dumb, I simply nod for him to continue.

"She was violent and mean, and I've never met someone who could be so evil and not be a Revenant at the same time. She drilled it into our heads that phoenixes were a blight on this world, and it only got worse after your parents turned. Father tried so hard to temper her, but... It's the hardest thing in the world to hate someone who is already dead."

Cam brushes away the tears with the back of his hand, pausing his story to take another fortifying sip of bourbon.

"I lied to everyone when I came back. It wasn't the phoenixes who killed my parents. After my cousins were hit, I went to check on them like I said, but when I got there... my mother had turned. She was eating the flesh of children. Children, Ash." Cam covers his mouth with a hand, trying to hold in a sob.

"And my father was letting her. He was just letting her do it. Do you know what it feels like to have to send your mother to Hell because she was just that evil? To know my father stuck by her, even though she was such an awful woman? I took her head." He sniffed, and then took a deep breath.

"I took her head and killed them both and then I set their house on fire. And I blamed them all—every single one of those winged devils, even though it wasn't them. It was me. And I am so *angry* that Olivia is none of that, and I can't figure out what is killing her. Olivia has been nicer to me than my own mother. She has loved me and treated me like I was special even though I am probably the biggest asshole in the known universe. I know we won't live much longer after they go, but it's going to be worse than losing a limb for me. I wanted to tell you I'm sorry for how I've treated you before it's too late. You are my family, and I have been no better to you than the woman who bore me. I am sorry, cousin," he ends on a whisper, the poison he's been holding onto finally pouring out of him.

I say the only thing I can.

"I forgive you," I tell him, amazed he has divulged this much about himself. Cam has always been almost one-dimensional to me, but now I can see he is more than the foul-tempered jerk he presented himself as. This hurts my heart more. I have discounted him as nothing more than a nuisance, and I am soundly ashamed to know he has endured probably more than he will ever say.

"We should have been like brothers, Cam," I murmur. "Better late than never, yeah?"

He nods and sips his bourbon again. We lapse into a comfortable silence for a while before John opens the double doors to the bedroom. His face is destroyed—there is no better word for it.

"I need both of you to get Aurelia for me," he rasps, and Cam and I spring to our feet.

"She's not—" Cam starts, but his voice catches.

"No. Not yet. But I haven't even asked for her help. If she can see what's hurting Olivia, if she can help... we need to utilize her gifts," John explains. "I have kept this under wraps too long."

Why didn't we think of this earlier?

"Is West still with you and Evan?" I ask, making sure

John is covered while we are gone, my guardian instincts kicking in even at the end.

"Evan is sacked out on the chaise, and West is passed out on the floor beside her. I'll wake him up if that'll make you feel better."

"If you wish, sir," Cam concedes.

"Oh, please," he counters, leaning heavily on the door. "I've been putting you boys through hell for these last few months. The least I can do is make sure I'm covered."

"Come on, we knew you were an asshole before we signed up," Cam fires back. "Comes with the job."

John inclines his head with a wan smile and turns, heading back into the bedroom. I look at Cam and we both nod, blackness surrounding us as we travel back to the house in Grand Lake. I have traveled this path so many times over the last few months; I don't need to concentrate on getting there. In just a few moments, we appear in the middle of the game room next to John's favorite chair.

"Are you going to be cool?" I ask Cam.

He grimaces in chagrin and gives me a grumbled, "Yeah."

Since the game room is empty, we search the rest of the house, looking for Aurelia. Well, Cam is searching for Aurelia. I am thoroughly failing in my endeavor to keep away from Mena and can't help but search for her instead. My body's clawing need to find her courses through my veins, overriding every other thought.

My resolve to leave her alone lasted all of two hours.

I am a pillar of strength.

It's instinct that helps me find her. Like an ironclad fist wrapped around my heart, it pulls me, tugs me through the house to the pale wooden door of a bedroom. I know she's there. It takes all my strength not to travel to her side, not to break this door in, to calm myself down and politely knock on the rough pine boards that make the handsomely crafted door. I rest my forehead on the cool wood.

My first knock is faint—no one would hear it even in the stillness of the house. My second one a minute later is only marginally louder, but the door opens, and I'm unbalanced for a moment. Not just from the door moving in front of me, but the sight of Mena upright and walking.

She stands tall, only three or so inches shorter than me. Her board-straight, dark mahogany hair is down and long, almost brushing her elbows. Her slender limbs are covered in a thin, open-weave, green sweater with sleeves so long they cover the heels of her palms, and with a collar so wide, it falls off one shoulder, exposing two, thin, delicate black straps, and a scar on her neck I hadn't noticed before. It's a silvery almost blue that looks the most organic of all her scars. It spans the length of the slim column of her throat and has an eerie resemblance to a lightning strike—a single jagged bolt stretching to her collarbone and the forked tines reaching into her hair like fingers.

It takes a minute for my eyes to move from that beautiful, yet haunting scar and take in the rest of her. She is wearing jeans that flatter the gentle swell of her hips and flat open-toed sandals on her feet. She looks casual and relaxed, an ease to her I haven't seen before. It still shocks me how fast phoenixes heal. Half a day ago, she couldn't even walk, and now she stands tall and proud, and so beautiful it blanks my mind and steals my breath.

"Is there something you need, Asher?" she asks softly, her expression worried, but also open and searching.

She's happy to see me, I think, and my heart does a nice little double bass tap against my ribs.

"Uh... are those new clothes?" I ask lamely. Considering she's worn nothing but a hospital gown in my presence, I sound like a fucking moron.

She gives me a look that tells me she agrees and says, "Yes. Evan got them for me in Oregon, evidently.

Somehow she knew my sizes," she ends with a slightly uncomfortable shrug.

"Good, good. Do you know where your sister is? John needs her help," I blurt.

Her face falls, looking hurt for a moment before wiping her expression clean. When she speaks, her tone holds just a hint of pain, and I feel like an asshole. She can't think I don't want her. Not when my default mode around her toggles between stalker and possessive asshole.

"She's training with Aidan in the gym," she says, her voice flat.

Jesus. She seriously must think I don't want her. I have to fix this. I have to. I can't let her think... I have to make her see it. I know it is the bond that draws me to her, but it isn't what keeps me here. It's her quiet strength, her worry for a stranger whom she might have hurt, it is the way she seems to have picked herself up and dusted herself off from nearly a lifetime of adversity.

It's all that is her that keeps me. That makes me know that this is what love must feel like.

Less than a day. How can I care for—no, love—someone in less than twenty-four hours? How can I fall this far this fast?

So much for staying away from her.

The knowledge that keeping myself from this woman is no longer an option hits me like a fist, and I struggle to pick the thread of the conversation back up again.

"I guess he's trying to get her back for smacking him on the head with that bokken," I joke, trying to put the smile back on her face.

"She hit him in the head? A wraith? Aren't you guys supposed to be harder to fight?" she asks, the worry for her sister puckering her brow.

"We are. Your sister is deadlier than any wraith I've ever met," I reassure her. "She put our King on his ass the last time they sparred. I'm not worried about Aurelia at all."

Mena wrings her hands. "I didn't realize she was so… adept. The Aurelia I knew so long ago couldn't hurt a fly. Well, she could slay one with her sharp tongue, but a fly could kick her ass."

"Yeah… not so much now. Do you want to come with me to get her?" I ask, even though I think she'll say no. I'm shocked when she steps from the room like she's jumping off a cliff.

"We're just going to walk, right? None of that swirly black smoke stuff. Because that was unpleasant," she says, her nose scrunching into a wince.

"Yeah. Traveling takes some getting used to. We can

walk if you want," I concede as I grab her hand. I don't hesitate or flinch, touching her as I would anyone else.

Except I don't want to hold anyone else, don't want to love anyone else.

I'm certain however long I have left on this earth, I'll never love anyone as much as I love this woman.

9

MENA

Staring at him in shock, I let him lead me down the hall, not coming out of it until we take the first steps down the staircase, when I have to watch my footing so I don't slip. It takes until the blood comes rushing to my cheeks and my heart decides it wants to trip out of my chest before I remember I'm staring at him like a moron. Dropping my gaze, I try to remember if I've ever felt anything close to this.

His hand is rough and warm, and I'm so happy I didn't shock him that my knees go rubbery. I never thought this was possible for me. Simply holding his hand, my fingers tangled with his, is farther than I've willfully gone with anyone. I've never dated anyone, never been close to anyone. I'm one hundred and eighty years old, and I've never even had a boyfriend.

How pathetic am I?

My joints quit aching after an incredibly relaxing bath in a tub the size of a small swimming pool. Aurelia spooned in some lavender salts from a giant cork-topped canister and left me to it. Well, she left me to it after I gave her the look of death after she offered to wash my hair like I was a toddler.

After I got out, my hip had finished healing, even most of my bruising was gone, and I could walk around for the first time in a long time. It is amazing how quickly one can heal if they are fed and not repeatedly reinjured. I got to primp and play with the makeup—not that I put much of it on—and brush my hair with something other than my fingers. After the relative metric ton of conditioner I used on my hair—that was possible. I felt pretty for the first time in forever, and I felt better after I saw the outfits Aurelia laid out for me on the bed. I'm not sure how Evan knew my sizes, and I shudder to know how she knew what my bra and undie sizes were.

Now, here I am, holding hands with undoubtedly the most handsome man I've ever met, and I can't trust it. It's too good too soon.

The incredible rush turns sour in my belly, and by

the time we get to the gym, I'm cold again. It stings after the warmth and happiness—so much it steals my breath. There is this emptiness growing in my chest—so deep and wide I don't think it'll ever get filled.

I need to enjoy this time. I need to clutch every second to my breast and keep it there for as long as I can. I won't get very many more moments like these, and it doesn't matter if they're real or fake.

They'll need to last me a long while.

My feet reach the final step of the last staircase trailing behind Asher, my hand still twisted in his and I see Aidan and my sister dancing around each other on a blue mat. The pair of them hold wooden sticks shaped like swords—bokken if memory recalls—and my sister looks like a ballerina, spinning and stepping out of Aidan's way as he tries to get in a hit. Rhys sits on a nearby bench, laughing so loud I can barely hear the music blaring from the tiny speakers at his feet. Aurelia is completely unscathed, but Aidan's nose is bloody. He's also listing a little to his right, nursing a broken rib or two by my guess.

Asher whistles and the combatants lower their weapons, but when Aidan tries to leave the mat, Aurelia smacks him on the shoulder with her sword. Aidan rolls his eyes before turning and bowing to my sister and then stows his weapon on a long wall filled with what looks like every knife, gun, and sword ever made.

"What's up?" Aurelia asks, eyeing our joined hands, her face blank.

"John wants you to see Olivia. He thinks maybe you can figure out what's wrong with her," Asher informs her, but he does something strange then. He tightens his grip and puts our joined hands behind his back, taking a step in front of me, positioning his body slightly in front of mine.

"Asher, what are you doing?" I murmur. "She isn't going to hurt me."

He turns his head, casting his gaze back at me, giving me such a look of pain and anxiety, I can't help but be confused.

"No, she's not going to hurt you. She's going to take you away from me, and I don't want to let you go yet," he admits.

My heart tries to beat its way out of my chest before dying a slow, agonizing death. He's going to let me go. I shouldn't care, because at some point I'll be leaving, but... it still burns.

"But you will let me go," I say, sounding almost like an accusation.

"I suppose at some point I'll have to. But it doesn't

have to be right now, and it doesn't have to be today." His low voice is almost pleading.

I do the only thing I can. I lie.

"I'm not going anywhere," I murmur, and the expression of relief on his face is almost enough to cure my bleeding heart. And if it weren't bleeding out from the lie that I just told, it probably would have.

"Good," he says.

"Asher," Aurelia calls.

He tears his gaze from mine to study my petite but menacing sister.

"If you hurt my sister in any way, shape, or form, I will set you on fire and smile while you die screaming. Do you understand?"

Rhys pipes in from the bench, leaning his body to the side to be seen around Aurelia. "And I'll help."

Asher nods and smiles, not the least bit scared. I don't like them threatening him—especially when it will most likely be me hurting him—but Asher doesn't seem to mind.

Cam takes that moment to smoke into the room, and I slide a little farther behind Asher. His fingers tighten around mine, and the tension in my chest eases a bit.

"I talked to him. He should be nicer now," Asher says as he steps to the side, bringing me with him.

"Let's go. Maybe if you can find out what's wrong with Olivia… maybe there's still time," Cam chokes out, and Aurelia's eyes start swimming.

"I'll do my best. I'm ready. Let's go," she says, even though she's wearing workout clothes and no shoes.

"Shoes, Gorgeous," Rhys says as he tosses her flip-flops by her feet and grabs her hand as she slips into them.

"Cam, take Aurelia and Rhys. I've got Mena," Asher says as he turns to Aidan. "You coming?"

"Nope," Aidan says. "Holding down the fort. Give Olivia our love."

Asher pulls me closer, wrapping me in his arms.

Wait a minute.

I didn't know I was going.

The feeling of ripping apart is accompanied by the swirling smoke of his traveling from the relative safeness of the Black compound to the unknown. I nearly pass out when we settle on solid ground.

Mother of all that's holy, please let us never do that again, I think as I rest my forehead on Asher's chest, taking deep breaths to ease the pain from the traveling.

"Oh, my God, that is awful. Why do you people do that all the time? Christ on a fucking cracker…" Aurelia says as she puts a hand over her mouth, looking green around the gills. Rhys looks just like he always does, yet his brow is lined with concern for my tiny sister. He leans down and whispers in her ear, and Aurelia nods—taking a deep breath—and rallies.

"It doesn't hurt us. Quit being such a wimp," Cam teases, jostling her with his shoulder good-naturedly.

"Shut up, jerk," she grumbles, rubbing her belly. "Good to see you got the asshole out of your system."

"Anything for you," Cam grouses as he ushers us through a set of mahogany double doors inlaid with an intricate circular carving of a tree of life—well, the doors seem old enough, they *could* be from the tree of life.

The room beyond is dim, only lit by a single glass-bowled lamp on an accent table next to a chaise, loaded down with a sleeping West sprawled across the upholstery—his massive boot-clad feet resting on the floor on either side of the chair. Curled on his lap like a purring cat is Evan, softly snoring with her hair looking like a hurricane hit it—the curly blonde tendrils half-covering West's face.

John and who I'm guessing is Olivia are curled in the huge, beautifully carved walnut king-size sleigh bed, covers all but obscuring a tiny body, playing little spoon to John's big spoon. Two walls of the room appear to be floor-to-ceiling windows, the thick drapes drawn, obscuring the outside view.

Asher releases me for a moment to gently rouse John, but Aurelia's yell startles the room into wakefulness.

"Oh, my God! Every wraith out of this room right now!" she exclaims, her eyes turning a bright blinding white, heralding a vision that will likely steal her sight for several minutes.

"Why did you wait so long, John? Why did you wait to tell me?" she moans, one of her hands in a tight fist and the other gripping Rhys' so tightly it might snap from the strain.

Her back begins to bow like the invisible strings of Fate are pulling her chest to the ceiling so hard her toes start to point, bending her body further and further. Her head makes a slow ticking motion as her eyes stare off into the distance—seeing things that have yet to be. I hope she sees something she can prevent because her expression is more than a little grim.

Grim would be a step up from this.

This is devastated.

This is agony.

This expression is hell.

I have to snap her from whatever hell she's seeing. From the little bits I've gathered, the last few weeks of her life have been awful. She doesn't deserve more. Her Aegis is barely visible, and I find it almost funny that I hadn't noticed it before now. To me, it is very nearly cute in how small it is. How small and faint, it is barely visible to the naked eye. It isn't hurting Rhys, merely coating him in the soft blue netting of electricity, but he looks afraid to move, so I do the only thing I can.

In the chaos of people jumping from their slumbers and John starting to yell in objection, I grab Aurelia's wrist and pull her out of Rhys' grasp, rocking her head a little. Her Aegis pulls mine from my skin, sucking a bit of my energy before her eyes dim and she takes a long slow blink.

"Thank you. That was bad. Oh, no…" she mutters as she puts a hand to her mouth.

Her face is an awful grayish-green and Rhys gives her a nearby trash can just as she plops her butt down on the carpet and loses whatever she had in her stomach.

"You okay, Gorgeous?" Rhys asks as we both kneel down next to her, and in response, she heaves a second time, gripping the trash can like a lifeline.

"Jesus, baby. It's okay, I'll be okay," he murmurs as he rubs her back.

"Poison… She's being poisoned," she gasps in between heaves. "Get all the wraiths out of the room. Don't let them touch her…" she says, the words coming out in halting sobs.

"How? How is she being poisoned, Ari?" Evan asks, and her voice sounds like a car crash—all twisted metal and broken glass.

"I ca-can't tell you. You'll touch it. You'll get sick. You can't get sick. You have to—you have to le-leave. Everyone has to leave," she moans, her eyes squeezed shut, her breaths sounding like they are being ripped from her lungs.

"Clear the room," West says as he grabs Evan by the waist and Asher yanks Cam by his bicep and drags them out. Evan struggles, begging to stay, but West tightens the band across her stomach and hoists her over his shoulder in the last few feet.

Through all this, even with the chaos and her daughter screaming at the top of her lungs, Olivia doesn't rouse. She doesn't move. Beneath the pale-blue down comforter, she looks like she's barely breathing.

"Tell me," John orders. "Tell me what is wrong with my mate!" His face is ravaged, tears clogging his voice and racing their way down his cheeks.

"You can't touch it," she pleads and only begins speaking again when John nods.

"There's Bixbite in the locket, and the locket itself is protected by a spell. It's draining her. I need you to help Olivia to sit up and lean her forward. Try and get the necklace to hang forward. Mena. Shield yourself. Get her locket. Do-don't be gentle, and don't to-touch the pendant. Only the chain. Do you hear me? Even you could die touching that pendant," Aurelia gasps out the last words as she starts shivering.

"I don't know how to do that," I hiss. "What if I kill her?"

"Try," she growls through gritted teeth. "You're the only one of us who can do this and not fucking die. You are the only one of us who can save her life. Just. Do. It."

Closing my eyes, I take in a huge breath trying to steady myself. No one is going to die.

I'm not going to kill anyone. I won't.

I loosen the reins on my Aegis—just a tiny bit—just enough to feel a surging warmth coat my body. It always feels so good in the beginning. But then I have to leash it again, and it's like a shoe that doesn't fit. First, it's just uncomfortable, and then it's blisters and blood and broken bones.

John is so careful with Olivia, and now that the covers aren't concealing her face, I can see just how sick she is. Her skin is a pale unlined alabaster, but her pallor is almost gray, highlighting the fact that her hair is a brilliant white that only blonds get when they age. She is unresponsive, rail-thin—not that I can talk—and her pale-pink nightie hangs from her shoulders in great gaping sweeps of fabric.

Then I see it: an oval, antique silver locket engraved with scrolling leaves and tiny roses. It's so lovely, but I can feel the evil pouring from it—one better, I can see it —a putrid red and swirling black. Staining the locket, staining the skin of her chest, staining her light.

I don't register when the door opens, I'm still watching the necklace like one would eye an angry snake, but when Asher's fearful growl reaches my ears, I know I have to act. Wincing as I reach for the chain, I grip it with my fingers as I rip it down, breaking the clasp. As soon as the clasp breaks, Olivia takes a deep breath.

Relief swamps me until, out of the corner of my eye, I notice Asher move with purpose toward me.

He's not supposed to be here. This thing, whatever evil it holds in its depths, will hurt him. I know it. So I do the only thing I can. I take off running toward the window, tucking my head and shoulder as I hit the drapes, the glass breaking around me.

It takes less than a second to realize that the house sits atop an enormous mountain at the edge of a cliff, and I am free falling to the earth.

Oh. Shit.

IO

ASHER

Trying to hold onto a pissed-off, scared-out-of-his-mind Cam is like trying to grip a wet fish—fucking impossible. West is no help because Evan has gone from the focused, linear-thinking, happy-go-lucky woman I've known all her life to a half-mad she-cat on steroids. Forcing Evan to do anything is like signing your own death warrant, her destructive abilities able to level entire cities. Maybe more now that she's older.

West is attempting to calm her down gently, but he's not making much headway.

I'm more focused on keeping everyone calm, but I feel this pull, this hook in my chest, and I can't stay downstairs playing babysitter. Out of everyone, I should be the staid one. I should be the one that is constant—that follows orders—but it's me who breaks rank first and heads upstairs before anyone can grab me.

Something is wrong. Mena is in danger—I can feel it in my bones.

For some insane reason, I take the stairs instead of traveling, and when I open the doors, I vow to regret that sixty-second trip for the rest of my life.

I don't remember growling or moving, but when Mena looks up at me, I'm already trying to get to her—trying to get her away from that darkness clutched in her fist. I see the decision cross her face as soon as she makes it. She'll do anything to save the people she loves.

Somehow, some way, that now includes me.

No, no, no!

"Mena!" I roar, forgetting my purpose, ignoring my oath to John, only knowing that I'll follow her down to the depths of Hell if I have to.

It takes less than a millisecond to process the room. I see it, but then again, I don't. Everything is on the periphery of my mind. I know John and Olivia are there. I know she's breathing. I know John is alive. I know Aurelia and Rhys are gaping in shock at the broken window. Rhys is standing, moving to help, but I'm not sure what good a phoenix with clipped wings is going to do.

I pass them all like they're standing still and dive out the window behind the woman who holds all that is left of me.

My power rises to my skin like a flash flood—rumbling, rushing, surging through my pores. The blackness of the smoke coating my skin like an oil slick is at odds with the morning sunshine, cutting the shadow of the mountain like a knife. She is falling fast, the fabric of the drapes she took with her floating away on the breeze like a ribbon in the wind. Mena twists and tumbles in her descent, but I don't hear her scream or cry.

And still, she plummets.

I've never felt as helpless in the three hundred years I've walked this earth as I do at this moment. Following her as she falls, I wonder if I should try to catch her or if I should attempt to grab her. If it will kill us both.

As I'm pondering our imminent death like a spineless pussy, she decides to save herself.

The bright-blue light of Mena's Aegis shines like the surface of the sun as she phases midair, her wings sprouting from her back with a great wrenching scream of agony—the first sound I've heard from her through the wind rushing past us—and my stomach twists. Her wings catch the air, buoying her, and I fall past her for a moment before I smoke out from my descent, reappearing at the bottom of the gorge. At the base of the sharp, craggy cliff, a thin ribbon of a stream slowly widens to a small river as it descends over the rest of the mountain. River rocks of every shade of teal, amber, and magenta cover the shore.

I watch her as she flies. Her wings are beautifully fragile and match her better than I could have imagined. The feathers are a vibrant turquoise at the tips, darkening to rich cobalt, and then to the softest blue-black I have ever seen in my life. I've never seen wings like hers. Most adult phoenix wings are red, orange, or yellow, never blue—and their flames are never this color. And then I understand. Her wings, her fire, they are all the blue of her Aegis.

Mena doesn't fly straight to me. In fact, when she lands several feet away, the frustration on her face tells me she wishes I hadn't followed. If I wasn't sure of her feelings at the moment, when I step closer, she growls at me to get back, her wings fluttering like a bird's in agitation. Her windblown hair flows wildly down her back, and her ripped sweater hangs from her shoulders, exposing the black camisole underneath. She drops the locket to the rocks at her feet, shaking out her hand as if she's trying to get feeling back into a sleeping limb.

I feel the pull again, the need to go to her, but her growl turns feral.

"I told you to. Get. Back. This is poison. I have to destroy it. Now, back up, Asher," she grits out through clenched teeth.

"I don't want to hurt you." This is a whisper she probably didn't mean for me to hear.

I realize now she's barely holding onto her Aegis. I move back another fifty feet, moving slightly behind a large boulder, and even though that might not be enough, I can't make myself move another inch away from her.

The veins of her power trace over her skin, glowing brighter as she focuses. An orb ribboned with the same threads of her power blooms around her, creating a shield of electricity.

Then, white bolts of light surge from her fingertips, hitting the locket with enough heat and energy, I stumble back on a foot, so I'm not knocked over from the strength of the blast. River rocks fly like shrapnel from a bomb as her bolts of energy slam into the ground. The debris falls all around, but nothing gets within five feet of her before it roasts to a cinder from her shield.

"Is it dead yet?" I call from around the rock, but she doesn't answer.

Only when she drops her shield—her body sagging slightly in the process—do I go to her. I don't go slowly

—one second, I'm a hundred feet away, and the next, there is barely a foot separating us. The heat from her flames should burn at this distance, but somehow, they don't. Staring into Mena's blazing amber eyes, I realize I need to hold her. Need to kiss her. Need her to know I'm hers.

Her expression grows worried, unsure but slightly relieved at having me near. But she doesn't break her gaze.

I know it then without really realizing how. Her flames won't burn me. Her Aegis won't hurt me. I'm in her heart just as much as she's in mine and that makes all the difference. The Fates put me on her path, and somehow—some way—they're paving our way.

This clawing need fills me, and I can't hold back anymore. Doing my best to go slowly, I cup her face in my hands, grazing the soft skin of her cheeks with my fingertips. Mena's eyes close as I press my lips to hers, her mouth opening with a gasp at just the right moment. When our lips finally collide, I slide my tongue into her mouth to taste her. She tastes like mint and woman, and the longer I kiss her, the more I want her— the more I need her. She moans, and it spears through me, straight down my spine to my dick.

Jesus.

Mena's hands curl into my shirt at my waist, and if

my eyes were open, they'd be rolling back into my head. Wrapping my arms around the small of her back, I tug her closer. Our chests collide, pulling a soft gasp from her lips, and I can't fathom a better sound.

Her fingers find their way to my cheeks, and then some wall in her crumbles because the kiss goes wild—all lips and teeth and hot gasping breaths. Our hands start roaming, and before I know it, I've hoisted her up, and her legs are around my waist. I find my hands on her ribs just under her breasts, and I have to fight with myself, so my thumbs don't go rogue and graze her nipples like they're aching to do.

Fuck. This is going too fast. Even though I don't want to, I break the kiss, resting my forehead on hers for a moment to catch my breath.

After several beats of silence, her eyes open, the irises still glowing amber, and it sends a thrill of satisfaction through me. I did that—I made that secret smile on her face, I made her breaths grow heavy, I pulled that moan from her throat.

She brings her thumb to my lips, rubbing the kiss into the lower one. She seems fascinated with them for a moment before her mouth drops to mine again, but she's the one leading this time. I'd let her set me on fire if she keeps kissing me like this.

When her tongue spears into my mouth, the taste of

her wrenches a groan from deep in my belly that seems to urge her on. Her legs tighten around my waist, and I feel the softness of her feathers, the heat of her flames cocooning us. I'm wrapped up like a bow for this girl and it's the best feeling in the world. She gently breaks the kiss, rubbing her lips across mine back and forth.

"I've wanted to kiss you since the second I heard your voice," I murmur against her mouth, and that pulls her gaze to mine again. Disbelief colors them as if she doesn't realize how gone I am for her.

"It was my first," she admits shyly, her head ducking into my shoulder so she doesn't have to say it to my face.

I'm glad she can't see the smug satisfaction on mine. I probably shouldn't be happy she hasn't had the affection she so rightly deserves, but I am. I'm pleased I'm the first person to love her.

Even if I probably won't be the last.

That weak thought sobers me, and my arms band tighter around her back as if someone were about to tear her away. I wish my brain would stop reminding me that I'm dying. That I don't get to keep her. I wish it would just let me have these few moments of peace.

"One hell of a first kiss, Princess," I murmur against the bare skin of her shoulder, doing my best to keep the sadness out of my voice.

"Really?" she asks as she pulls back, searching my face for a hint of deception—vulnerability stark on her face—and I know she finds none. That kiss was the best moment of my life.

I nod, and the smile I get in return steals my breath. Fates, I love this girl. Bond or no, mate or not, I realize at this moment that I'd love her anyway, and I can't seem to keep my lips from hers.

"We should probably stop kissing and let them know I didn't go squish," Mena says against my mouth.

"Probably," I mutter, and even though I don't want to let her go, I hoist her up so she can unwind her legs from my waist, and I notice that when her wings are folded and resting, the tips drag the ground.

"You want to come with me, or on your own?" I ask, and she shudders for a second.

"I'll go on my own. No offense, but traveling makes me want to vomit. I'm not doing it if I don't have to," she admits.

"That seems to be the usual phoenix response."

"I'll meet you up there," she says as she takes off with a giant sweep of her wings, the displaced air causing rocks and dirt to go flying.

She is beautiful as she flies, her spirit free. That is something I've come to crave in our short time together. I want to give her more of that, whatever way I can.

She circles and climbs until she's perched in the now-broken window, and only then do I go back up there, smoking in right beside her.

When I get to that room, I wish we'd never come back.

II

MENA

Fear, resentment, and rage fill the room. Clawing me, choking me, making it hard to breathe, making it hard to think.

Everyone is so angry.

They are angry at me for jumping out of the window. Upset with Asher for following me. Livid that Olivia was poisoned right under their noses, and no one noticed. The room is empty except for my sister and Cam. Olivia is being tended to, and I can't imagine what it would feel like if even one more person was here.

Aurelia is screaming at me, Cam and Asher are at each other's throats like they're three seconds away from having a death match in the middle of the king's bedroom, and I'm finding it difficult to be in a space with so much hostility.

I wish I'd never stepped another toe into this room.

I wish I hadn't phased back.

I wish I hadn't broken that last kiss.

I should have just kept kissing him.

I haven't let go of Asher's hand since he appeared next to me at the broken window, the wind whipping around us in the maelstrom of voices, screaming at the top of their lungs—their words lost as they tumble over each other. I'd already felt lambasted by Aurelia's tongue by the time he got there, and it only got worse when he showed up. My Aegis keeps spiking, and the louder Cam yells at Asher, the more agitated I become. I can't explain why, but someone threatening Asher makes me territorial and so angry, a thick, red film covers my eyes.

I feel my body heating up, and without letting him go, I somehow find myself in front of Asher, my teeth bared, and I can hear an ugly hissing sound—the first real sound to break through the thick buzzing in my ears. It takes me a second to realize the hissing is coming from me.

Cam's expression goes from murderous to wary in a second, and Aurelia's eyebrows shoot up her forehead so hard I think her face will break. In unison, they both take a generous step back.

"Stop. Yelling," I snarl, and they both nod. I turn to Aurelia and growl, "What, exactly, would you have had me do? You said it was poisonous. I took care of it. Stop bitching at me."

"And you," I say focusing on Cam, "stop acting like an asshole. For all anyone else knew, my wings could have been clipped or cut off entirely by Iva. I could have gone splat protecting you all, so excuse me if someone gave a shit about my fucking life. I didn't see anyone else at the bottom of that damn gorge, so if you have a problem with Ash making sure I lived, you can kiss my ass. Now, we all know my abilities are volatile at freaking best. I'm holding on by a thread here so I would appreciate a moderate tone of voice from here on out. Is that understood?"

Aurelia nods, appearing appropriately chastised, and Cam looks like I slapped him across the face.

"I'm sorry, Mena," he says, clearly contrite and the change in his tone is remarkable. "You did us a kindness, and I... I am proud my cousin was brave enough to make sure you were safe."

I nod in acceptance, deciding I've said enough, but it isn't until Asher whispers in my ear that I realize my fingers are sparking like downed power lines.

"Princess," he says as his hands find their way to my waist, "everyone is calm, you can drop your shield."

His warm hands on my body when no one should be able to touch me turns a key in my chest. I have to fight the urge to run my fingertips over my lips. I want to run away with him, I want to get out of this room and this house and just go.

Even if that is the worst plan I've ever had.

I want to get away from all these people and hostility and death. Because I feel death coming, it rises like an ache in my bones that something awful is just around the corner, and I want to grab Asher's hand and run.

"Right," I mumble and try to focus on calming down. Before it drops, though, Aurelia catches my sparking fingers. She's just as immune to my Aegis as Asher is, and it feels strange to have such gentleness after so long without it. I don't know what to do with it.

"I'm sorry I yelled. I was worried and felt useless because I couldn't get to you. You did the right thing, even if I yelled at you for doing it."

"It's okay," I say with a small wan smile and pull my fingers from her hands. "How is Olivia?" I ask, changing the subject from apologies and my shortcomings to something we should actually be worried about.

"She's awake," Aurelia murmurs, but I can see on

her face that isn't the good news we were hoping for. Their anger and fear make more sense now, and I can't help but feel an unexplained clawing sadness for this woman I don't know.

"Do you know who poisoned her?"

Aurelia's face screws up as she closes her eyes, reviewing whatever hell she saw. "I see blackness as an entity in my mind, but it keeps changing shape. They flicker and morph into someone else every few seconds —their faces are covered in black smoke. I think it could be several people, but I feel Iva's footprint here in the magic. It might be a group, but Iva was at the helm, and that scares the shit out of me."

That scares the shit out of me, too. A shivering tendril of fear snakes its way down my spine, and I can't stay in that room. I can't be anywhere near here. Bolting through the tree of life door, I hit a warm wall of a chest. When Asher's strong arms wrap around me, it is a war in my body over whether to run from him or relax into his embrace. My brain says "run," but my heart is driving this train, and my shoulders go slack.

"She's dead, Princess. She's not coming for you. You're safe," he murmurs soothingly into my ear, but he doesn't know. He couldn't have any idea what she's like. He's only heard the stories, but he hasn't seen.

"She'll come back. She always comes back. You

think she's done, but no. She'll poke and prod and needle. She'll tie you in knots only to unravel you and start all over again. She is the master of torture."

Shaking my head, terror rises in me again. "The worst agony in the world is letting someone think they're free only to steal the rug right out from underneath them. You don't know. You don't. You think you do..." I end on a shriek when I know I started with a whisper. His hands are gently holding my wrists, forcing them away from my face, and it's only now that I realize he's been trying to keep me from gouging my skin with my nails. My chest tightens, and I can't breathe.

I can't breathe.

"Shh, Princess. Breathe, baby," he murmurs, trying to calm me, but all it does is make me want to get as far away as fast as I can.

She'll come. She'll take everything away from me again, and then I'll kill him just like I killed my parents. I can't be with him. I can't stay.

"Let me go. Let me *go!*" I scream, yanking out of his arms, my body vibrating with fear.

"Mena-girl, I need you to calm down," Aurelia says from my left, and I have no idea when she got there. She sidles in next to Asher, and somehow the room is filling up with people again. I'm surrounded, and that flips a switch in me, changing me from terrified to livid.

"I'm leaving this room and this house, and you're not stopping me. Get out of my way, or I'm going through you," I growl, shaking. "All of you."

The circle around me loosens, and I make my escape down a rustic spiral staircase, my feet going so fast I have to grip the railing so I don't bust my ass on the wood. Asher smokes in at the bottom of the staircase, and the growl that erupts from my chest makes him step back.

"I'm not stopping you. I just want to take you back to the lake house," he almost pleads, holding his hands up to stop me. His eyes very nearly beg me, and in their sadness, I can't seem to tell him no.

"Okay," I whisper as I take the last few steps into his arms. He doesn't wait for me to change my mind and cups my face, dropping his mouth to mine, rubbing his soft lips against my mouth, startling a gasp from me. Traveling doesn't hurt this time, and I am uncertain if it is because I'm used to it or if his tongue dancing with mine kills the pain of every ailment I've ever had. It isn't until our mouths part that I realize we're back where we started: at the door to the room I woke up in.

"I know you're thinking about leaving. I feel it. Don't... just don't, okay?" he pleads as his arms band around my back, pulling me into the best hug I've ever had.

I can't help but rest my forehead on his shoulder and breathe him in. He smells like fabric softener and soft leather and the subtle, clean scent of man. The natural scent of his skin makes me want to run my teeth over his pulse point and nibble the skin there. It makes me want to bury my nose in his neck and breathe him in. It makes me forget, and forgetting is a luxury I've never had.

"Leave this house and this fight if you have to, but... please don't leave without me. I'll go with you. I'll make sure you're safe," he murmurs against my temple, his fingers burrow under my hair, and that sobers me.

He can't go with me.

He shouldn't be anywhere near me. How long could I possibly go without hurting him? Without killing him? Sure, he seems immune now, but what happens when I lose it again? I know I'm just a time bomb, ticking down to my eventual end. The best I can hope for is to reduce the collateral damage.

No, he can't come, but I nod, anyway. Lying with my body so I don't have to with my mouth, praying that when I leave this world, he forgives me for my dishonesty.

When I return to the safety of my room, I pull off my

clothes for another shower—the fear and bitter stain at the thought of Iva making me itch. I need to wash her away. I step under the still-warming spray, and my mind drifts away to my time in that cell.

"MENA." I HEAR MY VOICE WHISPERED IN THE BLACKNESS. I have been here so long, hearing my name when no one is there isn't new. I hear lots of things in the dark, and none of them are good.

But this voice is louder than my thoughts and the whispers of the dead that scream in my ears for vengeance. Louder than the echoes of Iva's taunts and my mother's screams of agony as I burned her to ash.

"Mena. I need you to listen to me. I need you to understand," the female voice says. "I have done horrible things. I have neglected you, and for that, I am sorry. But I will do anything to save this Legion. I will manipulate, and sacrifice, and I will kill to save them. I will sacrifice a few to save many. I will do horrible things for the greater good. And you can hate me for that. I hate me for that. And after all I've done, I will probably go straight to Hell once this life is finished. And I will accept it, because in this life I was given, I did not choose my path, but I accept my destiny. So, you can

dislike me, even hate me, all you want. I accept that. But I will save them. I will make sure that they are on the right path."

The female voice pauses, the faint but cultured British accent one I'm familiar with.

"I will bring them back from the darkness. But I need your help. I need you to stay here. I need you to endure this hell, and I will help you when I can. Your sister is coming. Not for a while, but she is. I need you to stay here until she gets you out. And when you get out, I need you to leave her and hide. People will come for you. They will try and steal you and make you a slave to feed their thirst for power. I need you to hide until Evangeline Marie Black has been made the Wraith Queen. When she's made Queen, go to her and help her. She will make sure Iva dies and stays dead. Do whatever you can to help her. And once Iva is gone, make sure you live. Live for all the time we stole from you and all the pain we caused. Stay strong, cousin."

That voice isn't mine, nor is it the tortured screams of my parents.

This one is real. Someone is in this barren room with me, and it is the one person who I thought of as neutral, if not a little evil.

Apparently, my cousin, Nicola, isn't as bad as I thought.

I NEED TO LEAVE.

I have to leave them all. I shouldn't have stayed this long.

And as these thoughts roll unbidden through my head, I allow myself just these few minutes to grieve.

12

ASHER

SHE'S GOING TO LEAVE ME.

That thought runs on a loop through my head, and I want to rip the house apart in my rage. I should go back to John and Olivia and see how I can help, but losing time with her tears my chest apart worse than anything I can imagine.

I want to do my duty, but I need her more than my next breath.

She's going to leave me.

And I can't remove myself from this hallway. Even when Aidan comes in behind me, I don't move my gaze from the door, separating me from the only woman I could ever want.

"John wants you to get back to the house, Ash," Aidan says gently from behind me, and I close my eyes to the battle waging in my head, resting my forehead on her door.

She's going to leave me. One way or another.

"I'll make sure she stays here, but you have to go," he says, and it takes a moment to realize I spoke my thoughts aloud. When I finally open my eyes and look at the man I've called a friend for so many years, he winces at my expression.

"I swear it, Ash," he promises, and I believe he'll try, but nothing and no one can hold Mena if she doesn't want to be.

"John needs you, Ash."

My gaze lingers on the door a moment longer before I travel to my King, dreading every moment I'm away from Mena. It takes seconds, but it kills me. I can't fathom how John could be away from Olivia for even a minute without losing his fucking mind. How can he stand this? This clawing, gouging ache. It rips at my chest, and I have to focus all my energy on not traveling back to her. I knock on the chamber door, feeling torn in two.

"Enter," John calls, his voice grave, and I open the carved doors for what seems like the last time.

"Sir," I say with a slight bow of my head when I

reach the edge of the bed. Olivia is sleeping in John's arms, and her pallor is much better than when I saw her last—a faint rose in her cheeks that has been missing for these last few weeks. Her hair is still white, and that's how I know she's still dying before John says a word.

"Bixbite. Fucking Bixbite," he mutters, tears coating his lashes, running in rivulets down his face.

When Aurelia said poison, she wasn't kidding. Bixbite or Red Beryl is one of the few poisons that can kill a wraith. Sure, many substances can harm us, but never kill. A gemstone in the beryl family can only be found in large enough quantities in one place—the Wah-Wah Mountains in Utah. Bixbite is so rare, the practical usage of it is almost nil. In fact, I've never actually heard of it being used except in cautionary tales told to children to get them to straighten up and act right.

I don't know how to respond, so I don't. I've never been a man to fill the silence when I don't have anything to say, and I'm guessing a "Gee, that sucks," won't be received well.

John sifts his fingers through his mate's hair, the white of her locks a shock of pale against his tanned hands.

"I release you," he whispers, not taking his attention from his mate's face.

Uh, what?

"I will not sentence you to die when you have found your mate," he tells me wearily. "That goes against everything in me, everything I stand for as a leader to betray our most fundamental law. I release you."

If he's releasing me, there is no hope for Olivia, no hope for him, and the pain is like losing a limb—blotting out all my questions of what is going to happen next. My composure breaks and my knees give out on the unforgiving hardwood.

John is a better father than the one I had, and Olivia is... she is the best Queen I could have asked for. These two souls are irreplaceable, and if I weren't mated, I would gladly honor my post and die with them. As it stands, I don't know who could fill their shoes. Evan isn't allowed to succeed to the throne without a mate—archaic, I know—and West has all but refused the mantle.

"How much time?" I choke out, the tears I'm hanging on to clogging my throat.

"A few weeks. Maybe a month. Aurelia wasn't certain, but it's not going to be today. We have some time to figure it out."

A month. So little time? I've lived five lifetimes, and

it isn't long enough. Now that I have a mate, a hundred wouldn't cut it, and it angers me that he's so calm.

"Get your mate, Asher," he says. "She needs you more than I do. All this mess can't be helping her, and now that we can guess Iva's involved... she needs you more."

Even though he is giving me something I need, it stings that he doesn't want me here. I give him what he asks for anyway no matter how much pain it causes me.

Old habits die hard.

I stand, bowing to my King, then I travel out of that room and that house back to Mena's door.

Aidan looks up from his book, perched on a barstool that he must have stolen from the kitchen island.

"Back so soon?"

"I've been released," I murmur, and Aidan flinches as if he's in pain.

He knows that means our King doesn't have much time, and he's eliminating collateral damage.

Aidan stands, his book forgotten, falling from his fingers. "How long?"

How long until we lose our leader, until we lose the one man that unites us all? How long until our whole world changes?

"A month at most." I scrub my hand down my face. "Trouble's coming. Can you feel it?"

"Yeah. West isn't going to step up, is he?"

"I don't know. But we need to be prepared for anything. I'm going to take a few days and see if I can get Mena to stay with me. I won't be any good to anyone if I can't get her to do that."

"Do what you have to, man. Just remember that kidnapping is a felony," he says, giving me a backslapping hug before he smokes out with his chair.

My way now clear, I knock on Mena's door. After a few moments of no answer, I try the doorknob. It turns smoothly, and I poke my head in to see if she's okay. When I notice the bed is empty, I lose it, slapping the door open hard enough to make it hit the wall and bounce back, smacking me in the shoulder.

I don't hesitate as I bust through the bathroom door.

When I find her in a heap on the floor of the shower, my mind goes blank, and my body moves on its own. As I open the door, I don't process that she's naked. I don't think about the deep scars gouged into her back. My hands find her shoulders, and I turn her so that I can see her face. It doesn't matter that I'm soaked to the skin, my blue button-up plastered to my arms and chest.

She's breathing. And conscious. And sobbing so hard her body bucks and shudders with them. I pull her onto my lap and just hold her for a moment.

She's alive. She's breathing. She's okay.

But then my brain finally catches up, and I realize she's bleeding from a gash on her brow bone.

"What happened, Princess?" I ask as I cup her cheek, inspecting the cut.

"I-I...can't deal with all of this. I can't...be... here," she says through gritted teeth, trying to stem the flow of her tears. But she's failing. She can't get ahold of herself and her body bucks again.

Right now, I just want to protect her—want her to feel safe.

"Then we'll go. We'll pack a bag, and I'll take you to my place. It's private, and we can get away from everything for a couple of days. What do you say?"

She seems to think about it for a moment, searching my face for an answer before closing her eyes, squeezing fresh tears from her lashes.

"Okay." She nods, her lips pressed so hard between her teeth, the edges turn white.

I pull on her bottom lip with my thumb until she releases the soft skin from the punishment of her teeth.

"But first, we need to take care of this cut," I say as I climb to my feet with her still in my arms, refusing to put her down for even a second.

She slips her slender arms around my shoulders, and I realize she may fear everything else, she may want to escape, but she'll escape *with* me instead of from me.

Progress.

Reaching for a towel hanging from a brushed bronze hook, I wrap the white terry cloth around her before setting her on the granite vanity.

"You never told me what happened," I press, unwilling to let it go.

"I slipped."

"That much I gathered. What made you slip, Princess?" I ask as I pull a first-aid kit from the bottom drawer. Unzipping the bag, I pick a few sterile gauze pads from their wrappings and start cleaning the blood from her face. The cut is already beginning to close, and I wait patiently while she fidgets with the towel to avoid answering me.

"I couldn't breathe," she admits, her lip trembling, "I was trying to figure out a plan. I was going to leave, but every time I thought about going, I couldn't breathe."

Her gaze pleads with me, torn between an apology and begging for help. I can't fault her because she couldn't leave. She feels the same pull I do.

"And how do you feel about leaving with me?"

Mena's lips curve into a shaky smile. "Like it's something I need to do."

"Good," I whisper, relieved. "How does your head feel?" I wipe the last of the blood from her freshly closed cut—the small mountain of blood-stained gauze on the vanity making my stomach drop.

"I've had worse."

I'll bet she has. I take in the exposed skin of her shoulders and arms, the creamy softness interrupted so frequently by the rough rivulets of her scars. I don't want to think about what she's gone through in that hell. If I do, I can't promise I won't stash her in a safe place and then find every person who lived in that house who didn't save her and torture them until they wish they were never born.

"Are your eyes going to turn black every time you look at my scars? Because I'm pretty sure that will put a damper on our relationship."

I feel like an asshole. My innate sense of justice is fucking things up all over the place. I'd hate it if she felt self-conscious about them, so I go about distracting her in the only way I know that has a chance in hell of working.

"My eyes are tied to my emotions just like yours," I say as my hands find their way to her knees, parting them to situate myself in between her bare legs. I can feel her answering gasp in my dick.

"They change when I'm angry or frustrated, or

aroused," I murmur in her ear. "My eyes turning black doesn't always have to mean bad things."

When I run my lips along the soft skin at the column of her throat, she grips my wet shirt in her fingers and pulls me closer. At this point, I'm cursing the godforsaken towel covering her and the roughness of my wet jeans against my stiff dick. But then her warmth filters in through the denim, and I'm finding it hard to think about anything but getting her mouth on mine. When our tongues finally collide, my fingers find that fucking towel, ripping it from her wet skin.

Her moan in response is almost more than I can take.

The rip of my shirt in her greedy fingers barely registers in my ears, but when the warm skin of her breasts hit my cool flesh, the very last vestiges of my control go up in smoke. Our hands tangle at my belt, and I'm so fucking turned on, I let her work the leather while I run my hands up her legs to find her slick, wet heat with the pads of my thumbs.

Wanting to taste her, I drop to my knees right there, grabbing her ass in my palms and dragging her to the edge of the vanity. Her palms smack the granite, bracing herself, and I can't fathom why that one little sound makes my whole body clench. Before I'm overcome just from the smell of her, I look up, checking her face. Eyes heavy-lidded, her mouth is open slightly as she sucks in panting breaths.

I was her first kiss. I'll be the first man to touch her this way, and while I want to take, I only want to take what she wants to give me.

"Say yes," I growl. "Tell me I can give you this."

Mena's eyes blaze amber as she nods. "Yes. I want you."

My mouth makes contact and the taste of her... fucking hell. Her sweetness on my tongue, the moans vibrating from her throat. All I want is to make her scream, make her lose herself, make her fucking come. I slip a single finger into her, and her back bows hard enough to snap a vertebra.

Nibbling at the lips of her sex, I work my finger in and out of her before giving her a long slow lick. Fuck, she tastes good. I slip in another finger, curling them as I concentrate the efforts of my tongue on her swollen clit. It doesn't take another second before she comes all over my face, wet and screaming.

After I work her through all her aftershocks, she's the consistency of wet spaghetti. Her damp hair is matted against her face and the mirror behind her head, clinging to the glass like a frog on a leaf. Her chest is flushed from her neck, past her breasts all the way down her stomach.

I have never seen a woman as beautiful as Mena in my whole fucking life.

I want to ask her if she's okay, but I'm not sure she's capable of coherent speech at this point, not to mention I hear the heavy *thud* of footsteps in the hallway, doing their damnedest to kill my hard-on. It doesn't quite work, because I just watched the love of my life come for the first time, and I have plans for her for the foreseeable future. And most of them require zero clothes and whatever sweet condiment I have in the fridge of my cabin.

I wonder if I have strawberry preserves in my refrigerator.

"I'd ask what that smile is for, but I have a feeling you'll show me when we don't have a herd of freaking elephants stomping outside our door," she rasps, and I realize she must have screamed loud enough to wake the whole house. Good thing the vast majority of the residents aren't here.

Shit.

My mind focuses on where everyone else is, and the bitter sadness comes rushing back, choking me. I rest my forehead on her thigh and force it to the back of my mind. My mission is to make sure Mena is okay. Screw everything else.

I stand, plucking her from the counter and carrying

her back to the bedroom. I give her a swift kiss on her rosy lips and set her on the bed. I cup her cheeks and dive in for another quick kiss.

"Get dressed and pack a bag. We're going on a trip," I murmur against her lips and promptly travel from the room.

No more interruptions, no more drama. Just me and Mena and a chance for her to heal.

13

MENA

It takes a few minutes to get myself together before I can A—stand up and B—focus enough to pack a bag. I've heard women talking about orgasms, but *holy shit...* I've obviously never had one. My sexual experience is limited to fade-to-black romance novels from the 1950s and '60s and some naughty translations of Shakespeare.

Well, that, and my first week under Iva's care.

I was only raped the once, and it kills me that my mind drifts back there after the beauty Asher showed me. It makes me feel dirty and soiled for an awful moment before I manage to shove it back.

In my soul, I know the difference between what that guard took from me and what Asher gave. I was a participant with Asher. I wanted it—more, I needed it. Fifty years is a long time to come to grips with sexual assault, and even though I didn't have anyone to talk it out with, I was taught enough about love to know what was taken from me wasn't my fault.

I didn't ask for it, and I didn't deserve it.

If I'd venture a guess, Iva probably coerced or brainwashed that guard to rape me—not that it stopped me from killing him when he tried to do it again or his friends when they attempted it. Even if they were coerced, I still don't feel a single iota of guilt for killing them, and I don't care if that makes me a bloodthirsty devil. I'm allowed to save myself from going through that again.

Heaven and Hell be damned.

What I do blame myself for are my parents' deaths. If I'd had more control, if I hadn't had to hide my abilities for so much of my life, I might have been able to save them. I might have been able to stop myself.

But when I cast my mind back to the deep pulsing agony of the aftermath of my assault, I'm unsure of any control I could have obtained in my long life that would have made even a little bit of difference. That scenario was orchestrated with only one inevitable outcome. Iva made sure she did the most horrible thing right out of the gate. She was just pleased she only had to do it once to get what she wanted.

At some point, I'm going to have to tell Aurelia, but I dread it. She's been estranged from them for so long, I'm not sure how she'll react when I tell her they've been gone from this earth for a very long time.

Will she hate me? Will she even care?

I dress in a sapphire-blue tank top, dark jeans that have a slight flare to the hem, silver T-strap sandals, and a thin, pale-blue, floral print cardigan. I'm not sure I'll ever be comfortable dressing in anything that doesn't cover my arms and back. The more I think about it, the more I want them covered with tattoos.

My sister had a good idea to take her pain and make it beautiful.

I find a brown leather weekender bag on a shelf in the walk-in closet, and pack enough clothes for at least three days, stuffing them into the bag haphazardly. On my way back from the bathroom with a full-to-bursting toiletry bag, the door bursts open. My sister looks fit to be tied, standing in the doorway.

"Is there something I can help you with, Aurelia? Or do you enter every room like a battering ram?" I ask as I stuff the toiletries in the weekender and zip it shut.

"You're leaving?" she half-yells, her chest heaving in a way that looks supremely unhealthy. Out of the two of us, she should be the most adjusted, but right now, I seriously doubt it.

"I'm taking a few days with Asher to get my head on straight."

"And what happens when the king dies, Mena? Because he will. Asher is the king's guardian and will die right along with him! I can't let you tie yourself to him only to lose him, Mena-girl," she says through tears, but I feel like she just shot me in the chest.

Staggering, I grip the bedpost to stay standing.

"Asher is going to die?" I breathe in a daze as I stumble back, my knees hitting the mattress as I plop down. A loud buzzing in my ears blots out her voice, but I don't need her to speak to know my decision.

"Yes," I say, my voice cracking.

"Yes, what?" she asks.

"Yes, I'd go with him, even if he was sentenced to die," I tell her, my voice barely audible. "Yes, I'd tie myself to him even if our days are numbered."

She looks dumbfounded for a moment before her voice goes soft, and she asks, "And how many of those numbered days are you going to deal with the fact that you were raped under Iva's care?"

"How do you know that? Did Rhys tell you?" I ask accusingly through tears, as I shove myself back to standing and take a threatening step toward her.

"Rhys knew?"

"He guessed. He wasn't with me for more than five minutes before he figured it out. If he didn't tell you, how did you know?"

"I'm not stupid, maybe?" she says, throwing her hands up before slapping them back down on her thighs.

"You shocked Rhys when he tried to touch you." She counts on a finger. "You wouldn't let Ian examine you without a serious pep talk, even though you had a major injury. Cam scares the shit out of you, but you don't fear Evan or me. You don't fear Asher either, which freaks me out. I don't know if it's the bond or him or you. I don't know if it's a good idea for you to be so intimate with him so early."

She heaves a sigh, dropping the hand that counted all her very good yet invasive points. "But none of that tells me how you're going to deal with it. I don't want you to go through any more pain than you already have. It's not fair to you."

"With Asher, I feel a warmth in my chest that has been missing my whole life. I feel... happy. I can see he cares for me. I can see it in his eyes and hear it in the hum of his voice. I *know* because he puts himself in front of me, protects me...he jumped off a damn cliff after me. So, I don't care if he has days or weeks or millennium.

I'll spend that time with him and deal with the fallout later."

Her dubious expression informs me she's unconvinced.

"What would you say if I told you I killed my rapist? And the fifteen other men that tried after him? That I'm more afraid of Iva than I am of any man?"

"I'd say that you were well within your right to do so and that you were smart," she says without blinking, and if there were ever a time to not bring this up, it would be now, but I have to tell her. If I wait, she will hate me for it.

"And what would you say if I told you I killed our parents by accident after I was raped? That I am more scarred by that than I am of the single element of torture that Iva used as a catalyst?"

Aurelia blinks once and hard.

"I'd say there are some things you can't take back, some things where a hypothetical just won't work. I'd say I need the facts," she says, and the shock and agony on her face makes me flinch.

Well, I opened this can of worms, I might as well tell her. Even if this is going to rip me to shreds.

"I was taken in 1965. I'd been working as a gentry at a funeral home. One night after my shift, I was walking home, and someone came up behind me and snapped my neck. I couldn't tell you how many days I was stuck in the dark, alone in my cell, before a soldier brought Mama and Papa in and chained them to the floor. It took days before they were awake, and we knew pretty early on it was because of me that we were there. Why else would they put an Aegis in the same room with Papa, if they didn't want to make sure that he wouldn't see a way out?"

Swallowing hard to dislodge the lump in my throat, I manage to continue.

"They tried to make plans to escape, but I think we all knew that we weren't making it out of there." I pause, taking a deep breath through the choking ache in my chest.

"T-then a soldier came in," I rasp, "and he r-raped me right in front of our parents on the dirty stone floor. And h-he made sure it *hurt*. Afterward, I t-tried to hold it in, but I couldn't—I couldn't hold it. When I woke up, Mama and Papa were ash, and Iva was sitting there clapping, congratulating me on a job well done." My short laugh is bitter through my tears. "Are those enough facts for you?"

Aurelia appears angry and lost, like I just took something from her, and I suppose I have. But I have enough guilt on my shoulders. I don't need hers, too.

She doesn't speak. She doesn't even blink.

"I'd say you've given her enough," Asher rumbles from the doorway, his growl a threat. He looks murderous, fully phased, and if I didn't know better, he seems to be ready to rip my sister limb from limb.

She shakes from her stupor and meets his hard stare.

He doesn't move his black eyes from hers when he asks, "Are you packed?"

"Anything else I need, we can buy," I say, ready to get out of this room and this house. I've done all I came here to do. I don't need to come back for anything.

He holds out his hand for mine, saying, "Then, let's get out of here."

I nod, stopping in front of Aurelia. "I love you, twin. Even if I didn't show it. I kept secrets to protect you and our family, and it kills me that you were mistreated because of them. I will regret my abilities and my part in our parents' death until the day I die. And I will love you even if you can't forgive me."

Moving around her, I snatch my bag, taking Asher's hand with my free one. As my freezing fingers make contact with his smoking taloned ones, a sharp tendril of dread snakes down my spine. Not from his phase or his anger, but the realization that is just dawning on me.

He heard every word.

The tears I tried to hold back crest the dam of my eyelids and fall unbidden down my cheeks. While he may be my safe place for now, our bond and our relationship will be scarred by this. I never wanted to tell him.

Other than informing Aurelia about our parents, I never wanted to divulge my shame to anyone else. Not that I thought I would be around people. I'd planned on going away in seclusion, avoiding relationships and anyone else who I could possibly hurt or kill. If Ash can't forgive my past, that plan might still be on the table.

He meets my gaze, his ink-like orbs piercing my thoughts and my heart, and we travel together, smoking out of the room in a swirl of black. The trip is short, and he releases my hand once we're outside to open the passenger door of a large coal-black vehicle with the word "Sahara" on the side.

"Get in, Princess, and let's get the fuck out of here," he rasps, his voice low, sending a surge of hope through me as I climb into the vehicle using the steel runner board to hoist myself onto the black leather seat.

Maybe I don't have to worry about him not wanting me. Maybe I don't have to let him go. If he only has so few days left, I'll spend every single second I can with him before I lose what's left of my heart when he goes.

14

ASHER

Focusing on the pavement in front of me, I carefully make sure the large all-terrain tires of my Sahara stay between the perforated yellow lines of the winding mountain road. I haven't said a word since I started the SUV, directing the tires away from the cabin and toward my house on the outskirts of Fraser. I'm holding onto my rage by a fragile, fraying thread.

I want to hate Aurelia for making Mena tell her what is most likely the worst sin on her soul, but I can't. I have this needling suspicion that if Mena could have, she would have kept that horror from me, she would have never told me a single shred of the terror she lived through. It makes me simultaneously need to hide her away to keep her safe and let her fly free. She has been cooped up in a cage for so long, I don't want to suffocate her.

I don't want to be another cage.

But I also want to go to the depths of Hell just to rip the flesh from the bones of the bastards who touched her and then kill them all over again. Slowly. Painfully. In ways that would haunt them and make the Devil himself shudder in horror. It scares me that I have that much depravity in my soul, but then again, it doesn't. John has done the same for Olivia, and for better or worse, he taught me how to be a man.

"How much did you hear?" she asks, her voice a quiet rasp in the silence of the cab.

"I came in at 'What would you say if I told you I killed my rapist?' and it was a fight to stay sane after that. I didn't want to eavesdrop, but I couldn't make myself leave," I admit, shifting my stare from the road for the first time since I turned over the ignition.

She's stopped crying, but her cheeks are still damp. I take my hand off the gearshift and reach for one of the hands trapped in between her knees. She weaves her slender fingers with mine, and I breathe a sigh of relief.

"Are you angry I heard?" I ask, hoping if she is, she forgives me soon.

"No. If the tables were turned, and I heard something so horrible happened to you, I wouldn't have been able to leave. You and I do our best to protect one another. I can't explain it, but I can't stand to see you hurt, and I know you can't live with seeing me in pain, either."

"I'm sorry you had to tell her that. I'm sorry it happened to you. I don't know how much guilt you have weighing you down, but I know you don't deserve to carry it."

"Maybe."

"No maybe. You were put in a situation where there was zero chance of a happy ending. You were put there on purpose by a woman who wanted to punish you for some dreamed-up infraction that had nothing to do with who you are as a person and everything to do with what you are. If the shoe were on the other foot, Aurelia would have been in the same boat as you in that cell."

"Maybe," she whispers, her brow puckered in a deep frown, and she is silent for a long while.

"You hungry?" I ask, trying to get her mind off all that has happened in just a few short hours since the sun came up. It's not too far past lunch, and I can't remember the last time I ate.

"Yeah," she mutters, sounding aloof, but she still rubs her thumb against my forefinger.

"We can stop in Granby to pick up some supplies before heading to the house."

"I'm not sure how good I'm going to be in public."

"Things have changed quite a bit since the last time you've been around other people. If you don't want to go in, you can stay in the car while I get what we need," I suggest, "and I can get something quick to make at the house."

Her mouth twists as if she's tasted something rancid, and she shakes her head no. I don't blame her. Leaving her in the car would sting, but I would have if she needed me to. I'm glad she doesn't want to be without me, as conceited as that sounds in my head. The shortcut to Granby is open for the next month or two until the snow moves over the mountain and this pass closes for the winter months.

I pull into one of the few grocery stores in this small mountain town and thrust the gear shift to "Neutral" before setting the emergency brake. Mena is practically plastered to the window, taking in the cars and signs and people.

Granby is a small ski town, with only about two thousand people in permanent residence with plenty of transient tourists in the winter months.

When I get out of the SUV and round the hood, she is still staring out the glass, slack-jawed. I try to cast my mind back to the 1960s to what this town might have looked like then. So many decades have passed in my lifetime that I have trouble singling out just one, and it makes me want to ask what her life was like before her capture—before her life went to hell.

"You coming?" I ask as I open her door.

"Yeah," she says, shaking her head and jumping down from the cab.

She shivers a bit in the brisk mountain air, and I wrap an arm around her shoulders. Our steps fall in sync, her long legs matching my pace with ease. I grab a cart at the entrance and start at the nonperishables, picking up paper products, a pack of extra light bulbs, replacement batteries for the flashlights and alcohol.

"What did you do before?" I ask, not elaborating on what "before" means.

"I was a gentry," she says absently as she inspects a package of disposable lighters as if they are the strangest thing in the whole world. "I worked in funeral homes or hospitals—though it is much harder to phase at a hospital—and ferried souls. I lived quietly, moving every five years or so."

We weave through the entire store, mostly to let Mena inspect each item that catches her eye, and I ask her questions when she's semi-distracted, learning little snippets of her life. The flu pandemic she lived through in 1918 New Orleans, the consumption outbreaks in 1880 and 1890. Most of her stories are about the work she did, but not much about her or her family.

Even peppering her with questions, Mena is still a mystery to me.

We load up with everything we'll need for at least a week at the house. Mena can't believe how many choices there are in products, from the different kinds of toilet paper to the fact that there is more than one brand of light bulb. When the store starts to get busy, her questions dry up, and she sticks even closer to me, wedging herself between the cart and the shelves, avoiding people as much as she can. I pick up the pace, grabbing the things I think we'll need and skipping the crap I know we won't.

The checkout process mystifies her, I can tell by her wide eyes and the eyebrows that have practically crept into her hairline, but she doesn't ask any questions. We leave after paying a sum that makes her eyes nearly pop out of their sockets, and load the Jeep to the brim before driving the last twenty-five minutes to my secluded home on the banks of the Fraser River.

I escape here every chance I can get, which isn't much. I come here so rarely, but having a house separate from John and Olivia was important to me. Maybe it's because I feel like myself here. I feel like this place is mine. It is a modest home in comparison to the Grand Lake cabin, with four bedrooms, four bathrooms, and a nice two-car garage to house my cars and toys. It is peaceful, my closest neighbor is maybe a few football fields away—a small foothill separating us from view. The river is low here, practically a creek in some places, but this year the snow melted late, and the waters rose higher than I've seen them in the last five years.

Mena assesses the house, a gentle upturn of her mouth letting me know she likes the look of my home. But she stops herself from crossing the threshold, stepping back off the porch and retreating to the open space near the Jeep.

"What's wrong?" I ask, worried.

"I need to bleed my power. I used to do it daily before I was captured. It helps me keep myself under control. I'd hate to blow up your beautiful house," she says with a self-deprecating twist to her mouth. "Where can I go?"

"Any place is good, there isn't anyone with a line of sight to this house. Just not too close to the Jeep, if you don't mind. Cars nowadays are mostly run on electronics."

"Duly noted," she says as she walks beyond the Sahara, putting about a hundred yards between herself and the SUV. She seems to consider it for another moment before walking just a bit farther and then she stops. I unload the groceries as she paces back and forth in the tall grass near the bank of the river. I put the milk, eggs, ice cream, and butter in the fridge and abandon the rest to go back out to watch her. She finally stops pacing and picks a spot a little farther from the water.

Then the light show begins, and I'm glad she's doing this during the day, so her Aegis is masked by the sunlight, scorching through the fat cumulus clouds. Her light strobes like a beacon, bolting from her in great wide arcs of electricity, reaching like fat fingers to the sky. They coalesce into a sphere around her body. It gets brighter and brighter, a jarring buzz coming from the beams before exploding in a sea of fragmented shards of light.

She stumbles, crumpling to the scorched grass like a puppet cut from its strings. The ground is blackened in a fifty-foot circle of ash around her, some of the gritty sand on the banks of the stream melted into a crackled glass. I don't think, I just travel to her, my feet burning from the residual heat coming up from the earth. I snatch her from the ground and move back to the porch before my shoes start to melt.

"I'm okay," she mumbles, her eyes closed, her head listing to the side enough for me to notice the bright-red blood coming from her nose and ears. She's breathing and talking at least, but it makes me wonder how much power she drained if she can't even stand.

"Princess, I need you to open your eyes for me," I murmur against her forehead, my fingers buried in her hair, clutching her to my chest.

"Gimme a minute. I'll be good in a minute," she haltingly mumbles, her eyes cracking open. "That was harder than I remember."

"I fucking hope so," I rumble. "Jesus Christ, you scared the shit out of me. Don't do that again. Fuck the house, and the truck and anything else that you could blow up. I only give a shit about you. The rest is just stuff. Never hurt yourself like that again, do you hear me?" I growl, my voice pitched low so I don't yell, but fuck, I want to.

She nods against my shoulder, but that just isn't good enough.

"Promise me. Promise me you will never hurt yourself like that again."

"I wasn't trying to this time. It's been a long time since I've drained myself. I've spent the last fifty years having Iva leach my power from me, sorry if I'm a little rusty," she grumbles back, sassy.

Iva drained her like this... My mind blanks. She's had to do that over and over again for the last fifty years? I can't stand it. I can't fathom the pain she's gone through. I can't imagine the agony of it.

I can't...

I cup her face and kiss her, rubbing my tongue against hers, hoping my kisses and my touch is enough to heal the weight of her scars.

15

MENA

I LOVE THE MINDLESS FEELING OF KISSING HIM, NOT HAVING TO think or plan or concentrate on controlling myself. In fact, he seems to want me more when I don't rein in my reactions. His response when my brittle control snaps makes me burn hotter, brighter. His groans and growls do something to me, giving me this pulsing ache in my lower belly.

I know we started the kiss off with me in his arms, but somehow, I'm now straddling him. I don't know if I moved or if he moved me, but I love the way my center lines up perfectly with the hard ridge in his jeans, pressing just right on my throbbing sex. I feel wild and out of control, and I love it without the fear or trepidation I thought I would.

The brisk outside air kisses my skin, lighting up every wet place on my flesh where his tongue has touched—the space just underneath my ear, my collarbone, the top of my breasts. I love that cold bite mixed with the hot lash of his mouth on my nipples, the texture of his tongue as it curls around the sharp points.

I can't hold in my growling moan—not that I'd want to.

He rests his head in the center of my chest for a moment, his heaving breath washing over my skin before looking up at me. His eyes bleed from their phased black back to his natural ice blue. He opens his mouth to speak but hesitates and snaps his jaw shut. I can feel the questions rising in him. I can feel his need to make sure I'm okay.

"I'm okay, Ash. I'm not afraid of you or this pull between us. I'll tell you if I'm not okay," I breathe across his lips, trying to dissolve the puckered line of his brow.

"Promise," he rumbles. It's not a question, it's an order, and if it were about anything else or from anyone else, I would balk. But about this? I only nod.

"I promise," I reassure him.

"Not just that. Promise me that you'll stay with me

—that you won't run. Promise," he orders again, but my response is less swift this time.

It isn't because I want to run from him, it's because I know his time is so scarce. I grip his face in my hands, stare into his worried face and give him the answer he needs.

"I swear, Ash. I'm not going anywhere," I say, and it feels truer now than it did when I said it this morning. It's not a lie anymore. Dropping my lips to his, we catch fire all over again.

My shirt hangs in tattered strips from my arms, and even though my clothing options are limited, I couldn't care less about the ruined cardigan or the tank top that seems to have disappeared or the bra that I heard rip just before his mouth made contact with my chest. I'm worried more about how I'm going to get his jeans off and how I can get myself naked without losing the hard press of him against my sensitive center.

My question is answered when he moves us, the hard, cold planks of the porch hitting my back, and I lose him for a moment before the crisp air meets my bare legs. I'm naked, my panties following the jeans as if they knew they weren't needed. The moment goes on longer, and I realize he is staring hungrily at my breasts, my stomach, my sex, my legs—his black gaze feeling like another caress on my skin.

Scars be damned, Asher wants me.

His expression says he doesn't even see them, but he gives me more when his voice rumbles a whisper, "Beautiful. So fucking beautiful."

Just that little bit makes me want to have him fill me right here. I don't need a bed or walls.

I just need him.

He still has his shirt on, and I need to know what his body looks like. I sit up, pulling and yanking the fabric until he gets the hint and reaches behind his neck to tug his shirt off.

His smooth skin is an unlined, perfect golden color as far as the eye can see. Built, thick-muscled, and solid. I've never felt small, being five-foot-ten, I've towered over men my entire life, but Ash makes me feel tiny, diminutive, feminine. I suppose I could feel fear, but I don't. It doesn't matter that he could probably toss me into the next county. I know he won't. I trust him.

I run the tips of my fingers over his chest, the hard ridges of his abdomen. My eyes must look hungry—he looks like a buffet—I only want him. Finding his nipple with my mouth, I torture a groan from his chest, which makes my sex clench. My teeth tighten on the flesh, and he grabs my face with his rough hands, and he kisses me, hard and hot, all tongues and teeth.

Suddenly, I'm not even a little cold. It was brisk on

the porch, but we've somehow moved. In the back of my mind, I figure he must have made us travel to a bedroom if the soft mattress beneath my back is any indication. *Handy.* I smile against his mouth and flip us, moving my lips from his to taste the cords of his neck, biting the pulse point like I've longed to.

I never expected I would have sex in the first place, let alone have it be so easy. And it is. I kiss and touch the places I think will bring him pleasure, and he does the same to me.

"Fuck," he groans, drawing out the word until its rumble meets my lips against his skin, pulling a smile from me.

He tastes so good. I wonder what else I can nibble that will make him make that noise. My nipples brush against the dusting of light-brown chest hair across his pecs, leading down the center of his abs, interrupted by the waistband of his jeans, and it sends a surge of wetness between my legs.

His pants need to be off. Now.

He must read my thoughts because his hands move from my hair to his belt, pulling the stiff leather from the buckle and moving to the buttons of his fly. I want to help him, but I am struck dumb at the sight of the denim popping open with each buttonhole, exposing the root of his cock. He's not wearing any underwear, and two thoughts run through my head. I wonder what he tastes like, and in the back of my mind, I wonder if it will hurt. But that last thought is fleeting.

God, I want to taste him, comes back through my brain, and I reach for him.

Our hands tangle at his waistband, pulling, yanking the denim from his legs. I'm not sure when his boots came off, but I'm not complaining. I take in the perfect, tanned flesh, the striations of muscles creating peaks and valleys of his broad chest, the abs and thick cock jutting up from between his legs toward his belly button.

I'm nearly coming out of my skin.

My inspection must go on too long because he's moving, picking me up by the cheeks of my ass and flipping me and then he's over me, dragging us up the mattress, moving in between my legs and I can't wait anymore. I meet his gaze as I reach between us, guiding him to my entrance, notching the head of his dick at my opening. Asher hesitates, his fingers winding their way into my hair, his coal-black eyes holding mine as his thick shaft presses slowly into me.

Making love to Asher is like I always knew it should be. It doesn't hurt, it doesn't feel wrong, and when his voice reaches my ears, I know.

"Mena," he whispers, and I watch his mouth as he

says my name, his full lower lip begging for my teeth and I oblige, nibbling it before kissing him for real.

He growls in my mouth as he moves, my hips rocking to match the rhythm of his, and I can't hold in the moan erupting from my throat, even if I wanted to. My legs wrap around his back, sliding him in even farther, touching a place in me I didn't know I had and didn't know I needed to be stroked until that very second. His dark eyes never look away from mine, and I feel them like a caress on my skin. He makes me feel beautiful and sexy, and the love and adoration in them touches an undiscovered broken part of my soul and heals it.

"More. There. Please," I beg, but I don't have to.

He felt me squeeze him, and he knows just where to stroke, he knows just how I need him to move. He sits up, bringing me with him and he gets even deeper somehow, his hands gripping my ass as he moves me, guiding me up and down his thick cock. My back bows with the feel of him, my breasts pressing against his chest, and then I'm coming, my orgasm hitting me so fast it's like a surprise, pulling a scream from my mouth before I can stop it. He moves us again, flipping me on my back, and he thrusts so deep I can feel him everywhere.

I need to kiss him. I need his mouth on mine.

Not want. Need.

My fingers find his hair and I bring his mouth to mine, kissing him through the build of another orgasm, this one bigger, longer. This one feels like it will break me in half, and all the while he's whispering against my mouth, "Jesus, Mena. Fuck, baby, that's so good, so good. You going to come for me?"

The question hits something in my chest because I have to answer him.

"Yessss," I hiss right before it hits me so hard I can't breathe.

I can't think. I can only follow the rhythm of his hips as his orgasm rolls through him, ripping a groan from his throat as his sharp fangs break the skin of my shoulder, but they don't hurt like I thought they would. Instead, they tear another orgasm from me, faster and harder than the rest, wrenching a scream from my throat.

When it finishes pulsing through me, I sag in his arms, spent, melting into the bedding. My eyes close on their own, sleep pulling me under before I can tell him something that I haven't been able to until this very second.

Before I can tell him that I love him.

I WAKE UP ALONE IN THE DARK, FEELING AS IF I'VE SLEPT FOR years instead of what I'm assuming is just a few hours. The moonlight filters in through an east-facing window, and I can make out a bedside table with a lamp perched on top. I hesitate before reaching for the light, wincing as I turn the switch. The bulb blazes to life, illuminating the room with a soft glow.

The bed I neglected to inspect earlier in our haste is an expertly carved sleigh-style, covered in a thick navy down duvet and crisp slate-gray sheets. The bed is decidedly rumpled, the covers mussed from our love-making and sleep. I love that I'm in the middle of the bed, not relegated to one side, the pillow I woke up with seeming to have been shared by the both of us.

The side table has a healthy stack of books on top. The rest of the room is clean and tidy, at odds with my thoughts of what a bachelor would be. Across the room, a comfy-looking reading chair has a soft flannel shirt hanging over the back, and I slip it on as I leave the bedroom to search the house for Asher.

"Ash?" I call, moving down a short hallway that leads to an open landing furnished with bookshelves and another reading chair. The dark wood of the stairs is bisected by a soft printed carpet, the pattern nearly indiscernible in the dim. The vaulted ceilings crest over a dark living room, windows spanning nearly floor to ceiling, silver moonlight filtering in through the glass.

I follow the sounds of pans clanging and make my way through the living and dining rooms to a brightly lit kitchen. Ash is shirtless, his bottom half only covered in loose-fitting flannel pajama bottoms and his feet are bare. He's stirring a wonderful-smelling concoction in a saucepan.

"You hungry, Princess?" he asks without turning, stirring the wooden spoon once more before switching the fire off, pulling the cast iron pan from the monster of a stove and resting it on a potholder on the concrete countertop.

"Yeah. How long was I out? I'm starving," I say as he moves to me, trapping me in the circle of his arms against the counter. My lips find his, and he kisses me long enough to reduce my IQ by at least ten points, only breaking the kiss when my belly lets out a roar for the steaming food on the counter. He chuckles and releases me, pulling down two dinner plates from the cupboard.

"I just got up a half-hour ago, but I think we were out for five or six hours." He shrugs. "How do you feel about breakfast for dinner?"

"I think that sounds excellent." I offer a genuine, happy smile. "What did you make?"

"Sunnyside-up eggs and my super-special sweet potatoes," he says, but I know the expression that's now on my face reveals my skepticism.

"Just taste it. If you hate it, I'll make whatever your heart desires," he says as he crosses his heart with his finger and holds up his right hand like he's swearing on a Bible.

He fills our plates and guides us to the wrought-iron barstools at the high counter of the island. Two eggs for me, four eggs for him, and the rest of the available space on his plate is piled high with dark orange sweet potatoes, diced red bell peppers and golden-brown chunks of bacon. He gives me a healthy portion, and after the first bite, I eye his plate, knowing I'm likely going to steal some of his after I fill my belly with every single morsel on my own.

"Okay, you can cook," I admit after my tenth bite. "What other talents do you have hiding under your hat, Mr. Crane?"

He smiles at me, and I can't recall his lips ever curving so far or him looking this at ease in my presence. I want so much for us to stay here, in this moment, in this house, away from the coming heartache. Just stay in this warm little bubble of happiness, away from the pain heading toward us faster than a freight train.

16

ASHER

MENA'S GIGGLE IS THE BEST SOUND I HAVE EVER HEARD, ONLY second to her moan. She's laughing at my stories of Aidan and Ian's antics—the brothers are always good for comedic relief. Their stories were needed after Mena explained why she couldn't tell me more about herself.

I'd started asking about her, about who Mena was apart from her captivity, and she couldn't tell me. Her answer when I pressed broke my heart wide open, and I couldn't fathom a life lived in such secrecy.

"I don't know who I am, Ash," she'd said, "Every memory I have has been a lie. Every single day was 'Don't run, don't yell, don't make waves.' I never had an honest reaction to anything before my capture. Every thought filtered through three layers of my parents' rhetoric, and the usual response was 'Don't speak and don't blink.' I don't even know what my favorite color is or what I like to do for fun."

I was speechless for a moment before I told her a story about how Aidan wanted to learn how to crochet and didn't want Ian to know so he tried learning it on YouTube in secret. He ended up getting his fingers trapped in the yarn and Ian had to cut him out of it, and then Ian taught him how to do it right. She giggled from start to finish, peppering me with questions about what YouTube, computers, and the Internet were. Then I told another about how Ian bet Aidan he could out drink him at a TGI Fridays in Denver. Somehow the bartender got roped into it, and she drank them both under the table, and they almost got arrested.

"How'd they get out of it?" she asks, as she leans toward me practically out of her seat. Her legs are trapped between mine, her bare knees brushing against the flannel of my pajama pants. Mena's willowy limbs have filled out a bit in such a brief time. Her cheekbones have lost some of their sharpness, her joints less prominent. Her skin is rosy, flushed with laughter and good food, and I give into the temptation of her smooth skin and run my fingertips up her thighs.

"Ash?" she calls, but I can't take my eyes off my tan hands against her creamy skin. The tails of my blue flannel shirt cover the top of her thighs, and I know there isn't a stitch of clothing underneath the soft cotton. The thought of her bare skin rubbing against the fabric of my shirt makes me want to bite her.

Just a little. Just a little nibble, maybe on the soft skin of her long neck, or maybe on the dark, dusky pink of her nipples. Maybe on the milky skin on the inside of her knee.

The thought of biting her reminds me that I completed our bond and didn't tell her what I was doing or what it means. I didn't tell her that my bite tied her life to mine just as John's is tied to Olivia's. I didn't tell her that my bite made her my mate. Made it so I could feel her heartbeat in my chest, feel her breaths in my lungs. I made it so if she ran I could find her anywhere. I should feel guilty, but I don't. What I did goes against everything I've been taught, and every bit of advice John gave me. But I don't give a shit. I felt it. She was holding a piece of herself back like she was staying with me for a little while and then she was going to go off on her own.

And I just couldn't let her go. But I have to tell her.

"I did something that is most likely going to piss you

off," I say, directing my gaze on my hands resting on her thighs.

"How do you know it's going to make me angry?" she asks as she rubs circles along my knuckles and fingers.

"Because I should have asked you first," I admit. "I should have told you what it meant before I did it."

"Okay," she says evenly. "What did you do?"

"I-I bit you," I say, finally meeting her eyes, reaching to the open neckline of *my* shirt, exposing the already-healed scar of my teeth marks on the meat of her shoulder. "I cemented the bond. I-I mated you, tied you to me. I knew what I was doing when I did it. I should have asked you, explained what it meant, but—" I pause, and I can't say any more.

"You were afraid I would say no?" she asks, tilting her head to the side, her eyes unreadable, and a cold finger of dread slices through me.

"I didn't want you to run and me not be able to find you. I didn't want to spend another day without you as mine. I didn't—" I break off.

"And there is no going back, is there? You made the biggest decision of my life for me, just like every single person has done my entire existence," she chastises, and I feel the guilt now. I didn't feel it before, and just like I vowed not to, I put her in a cage.

"I'm sorry I didn't ask," I admit, "but I'm not sorry I did it. I just... I just didn't want you to leave," I confess and pray—just pray—she doesn't leave my sorry ass.

"You should have asked. I would have said yes. Even though you are going to die soon. Even if I only got a few weeks of being yours, I still would have said yes," she says haltingly, her eyes filling.

"Only a few weeks? Do you know something I don't?" I ask, cupping her face in my palms, rubbing the tears away with the pads of my thumbs.

"The king is dying, Ash. That hasn't escaped your attention," she hisses, all pretense of calmness gone. Her eyes are flashing amber, but she holds onto her Aegis for now.

"And he released me from my post before I ever came to you, Mena. I would *never* have tied myself to you if I knew I was going to die. That would make me the worst kind of man. I would never sentence you to death just so I didn't die alone," I murmur, hating that she would think that of me, but knowing I deserve it for my high-handedness.

"You're not dying?" she asks, her body vibrating with either anxiety or fear or relief, and I can't believe she has been with me for this long without asking. Then it dawns on me. She thought I was going to die, and she still would have said yes.

"No, Princess. I'm not dying," I murmur against her lips and then kiss her for all I'm worth, cupping her ass in my palms and pulling her onto my lap. She doesn't hesitate to kiss me back, her tongue meeting mine in a not-so-gentle glide. Her teeth nip at my bottom lip as she digs her fingers in my close-cropped hair. I almost wish it were longer so I could feel her pull it. She's shivering still, but I know it is her need for me making her vibrate. I fucking love it, and I love her, and if I were to die in the next five minutes, she needs to know how I feel.

"I love you, Mena. I wouldn't have done it if I didn't love you. I just want you to stay, please just stay with me," I whisper, my voice clogged with worry and fear and love for this woman.

"I love you, Ash, and I'll stay with you," she vows, looking me right in the eye as she gives me the best gift I've ever received.

I couldn't stop kissing her if I wanted to—which I don't. I don't ever want to stop kissing her. I band one arm under her ass and the other around her back and hoist her tighter to me before standing from my barstool in search of a flat surface—any flat surface. The bar is too tall, but the dining room table—now, that'll do just fine.

Setting her on the dark walnut wood, I love that my

bride is sitting her bare ass on a table I hand carved. I pluck open the buttons of her shirt—my shirt—watching as each inch of her skin is exposed. I spread the fabric, revealing Mena's beautiful body, her natural curves finally filling out now that she is properly fed.

I trail my hands up her thighs, circle her waist and ribs in my palms, and then thumb her taut nipples. Her shiver brings a feral growl from my lips, and I pull the shirt off her shoulders, loving the look of my mark on her. I tug the shirt from her arms, and then she's done. With a ghost of a shy smile across her lips, she reaches in, and my cock is no longer trapped in my pajama bottoms. It is free, and in her warm hand, she's stroking me like she knows my dick belongs to her. I suppose it does.

I kiss her, pressing my tongue into her mouth, meeting hers before nipping her lips and moving down her neck over that lightning of a scar, over the crown of her shoulder. Tasting her mouth, her skin, moving to her nipples and her belly, gently pressing her so her back meets the cool, smooth wood. Her ragged pants just spur me on as I pull her ass to the edge of the table, notch my dick at her opening and slowly drive in to the root.

My pants are still half on my ass, but all I care about is the soaking wet warmth on my cock and her pleading moans. She scrabbles for a hold on the edge of the table for a moment before abandoning it to sit up, gripping my chin and moving it out of her way to kiss and lick and bite with those perfect blunt teeth on my neck and shoulder.

I pick her up and turn us, pressing her to the closest wall, ramming into her hard enough to knock the painting or frame or whatever-the-fuck off the wall. The sharp crack of the glass breaking barely filters into my consciousness before I'm pulled under again, lost in her moans and warmth and touch. I wanted to go slow, take my time, but I'm unbidden and unleashed, fucking her, stealing her breath.

She moans into my ear, "Please, God, please don't stop. Don't ever stop." And her words are my undoing. I reach between us, bowing my back just a little to make room for my hand, and I thumb her clit with firm pressing circles. Her body squeezes me, tight enough to almost hurt, and then she's screaming my name.

Before I come, I do what I should have done the first time we made love.

"Mena, I want you to be my wife, my mate, my life. Do you accept me as yours?" I growl my question into her ear, making her shiver in aftershocks.

"Yes," she whispers, and that is all I need to hear. My fangs lengthen just a bit before I strike, piercing her fragile flesh with my cutting teeth as I come unbidden of any guilt, harder than I ever have in my life.

She's mine. All mine, I think as a smile stretches across my face. I am—for the first time in my life—at peace.

17

ASHER

HER MOUTH FINDS ME IN THE NIGHT, WARM AND WET ON MY dick, waking me from a dead sleep. I let her play for a few minutes, loving her gentle sucks mixed with harder, longer ones, groaning at her long licks until I'm about to lose it. I haul her up my body, flipping us until she's pinned under me, and then I make her squirm.

I kiss all the spots I think could possibly elicit a moan from her, the delicate skin of her neck, the crown of her shoulder, the bottom of her breasts, her ribs, her hip bone, before flipping her over to her belly and making my way up her back. I nibble at the gentle swell of her ass before running my tongue up her spine, starting at the small of her back and ending at her hairline. Mena's hips roll, fitting her perfect ass right up against my dick, and then I begin my slow torture as she does her best to break my concentration.

I rake my fangs against the delicate skin of her neck, pinning her to the mattress and winding my arm around her middle and down to find her wet and ready. Her legs spread on their own, and I guide my cock to her opening, sliding into the slickness. I move slowly and stay close against her beautiful back, gently fucking her from behind as our breaths mix and mingle in the quiet of the night.

We never do get very much sleep.

The morning light streaming through the picture window brings me a slumbering Mena, hair wild with sex and sleep, her back cuddled to my front. She is completely naked, and even though I could wake her up again as I did many times last night, I don't. Instead, I opt to slip from the warmth of the sheets and make my way to the master bath to take care of business, brush my teeth, and take a quick shower.

I walk back into the bedroom with a wide white towel wrapped around my waist to find Mena sitting up in bed, the gray sheets clutched to her chest. Half of her face is creased from where she was lying on the rumpled sheet, hair shooting in every available direction, and she only has one eye open. And she is the most beautiful woman on the planet.

"Not a fan of mornings, Princess?" I chuckle.

"Nuh-uh," she grumbles, then yawns wide enough for her jaw to give a little *pop*. Her arms stretch high above her head, causing the sheet to drop, exposing her perfect pert breasts.

"I need a shower. I'm all... sticky. And I need coffee. And... hey! You already took a shower," she accuses with a pout once both her eyes finally open.

"Yes, well, one of us should make the coffee, Princess," I quip and her pout dissolves into a half-smile just before I kiss her.

"That sounds terrific, Ash," she says as she gives me a lingering kiss and slips from the bed to get cleaned up. Her ass gives a gentle sway as if she knows my eyes are glued to her backside, and it takes an enormous amount of willpower to not follow her. Throwing on some jeans, I half-button them in my laziness, setting out to give her another awesome meal.

After a day of lazy fucking on every single available surface—flat or not, horizontal or not—I get to the heart of her. How scared she was of exposure when she was a gentry, how much she hated shunning Aurelia. How her father taught her how to hotwire cars "just in case." How she wishes she had more medical knowledge because "The medicine in the 1800s was atrocious." But mostly, I got to see her smile, hear her laugh, and fall more in love with my mate.

"You made all these pieces?" Mena asks, amazed as she takes in my workshop nestled in the finished basement. I look at the sawdust-laden tables and the curls of shaved wood littering the floor beneath the carving table. The space is considerably less tidy than I normally keep it, but I left in a hurry the last time I was here. I've carved furniture for as long as I can remember. What started as a hobby as a child—anything to be outside—turned into my solace when my world went straight down the proverbial toilet.

Mena is staring at my most recent creation, a circular dining table with a tree of life carved into the walnut wood. The variation in the veining of the wood compliments the carved leaves, making them look like they are being ruffled by a soft breeze. I started it before Olivia fell ill, and it still sits unfinished.

"This reminds me of that gorgeous tree of life carving on the doors of the royal suite," she says in awe, and I can't hold back my chuckle as understanding dawns on her face. "You did the doors?" she asks in admiration.

"Yeah. Before life as I knew it shit the bed, I did

much of the furniture for different wraith families. Olivia likes my work, so she had me make the doors. This table was supposed to be a present from John for her breakfast nook," I tell her, and a wave of sadness washes over me.

Olivia and John have been such a big part of my life, I'm unsure of how I'm supposed to move on without them. Having Mena helps, and as if she can sense my swift change in mood, she wraps her arms around my waist and kisses the underside of my jaw.

Today has been one of the best days of my life. Just talking to her, getting to know her responses to the smallest of things, eases the burn in my chest at all the things she has been denied. Mena may not know what she used to like, but she seems to be making up her mind about things as she goes along. Cream and no sugar in her coffee, enough salt to start her own mine on her French fries, and an unwavering thirst for orange juice. I can't wait to see what she discovers she'll like next.

Her kisses are turning sensual, the gentle brush of her tongue against my pulse point sending all the blood to my dick, when the lights abruptly go out. The once-well-lit basement is black as pitch, the evening sky offering only slivers of moonlight through the narrow basement windows. Mena freezes, clutching my waist tighter before she tells me to hush. While a phoenix can't see in the blackness as a wraith can, her ears are much better than mine.

"I think the power was cut," she murmurs against my neck. The hair on the back of my neck stands on end as I phase without thought. I grab her close, ready to travel out of here when she stops me.

"Nicola told me this would happen," she furiously whispers in my ear. "She told me that people would come for me. They would come for my power, ready to drain it as Iva did. Make me a slave all over again. It's why I was going to run—on my own—to spare everyone, but if we run now, they will follow. I am too easy to find." This information would have been good to know before assholes started storming my house, but I can't yell at her. I really want to, though.

I would have run with her. Doesn't she know that?

Through the slight green cast of my night vision, her face is pained—beseeching—begging me to understand.

"Do you suggest we fight in this blackness? I can, but how are you supposed to see? And how will you fight? Do you have any training? Or are you going to rely on the power they crave?" My questions pepper her, rapid fire. I am so pissed at her, but I need the facts.

"I've spent the last fifty years in the dark, I can see

just fine. And if you think my father didn't teach me to fight, you are sorely mistaken. The only reason they captured me the first time is because they caught me off guard. If they want me, they're going to have to fight to get me this time," she informs me, her spine straight, her eyes glowing in the dim.

This is the strongest I've ever seen her, the fire that she has had banked for so long finally coming out to play, and fuck if it doesn't make me love her more.

"Weapons?" she asks, and I walk to the west wall, pressing on the shelving just so to release the lock on the false wall, revealing a small weapons cache.

She immediately reaches for a katana, snatching it from its pegs and unsheathing it to check the blade. Satisfied, she sheaths it and unravels the attached back strap to throw it over her head before tightening the strap over the middle of her breasts.

"Got any handguns? I'm shit with a rifle."

Who is this woman? I knew she was strong, but I did not know she was this much of a badass.

I hand her a Sig and watch as she mutters, "Those bastards are ruining my honeymoon," while she checks the magazine and chambers a round. She grabs an extra magazine and tucks it into her bra. She's not wearing much, just a thin, buttoned-up Henley and short pajama shorts, feet bare. I didn't even want her in my workshop with bare feet, and now she has to fight that way. *Fuck.*

I grab a Glock, check the mag, and stuff it in the back of my jeans as a backup. I'm not wearing much either, just jeans and a flannel shirt and no shoes. *Shit.* I grab a pair of Kukris, testing the weight of the blades before stealing a quick kiss from her.

"You stay behind me and stay close," I order, but I can tell she's only staying at my back to humor me if the eye roll is any indication. We move together, up the hardwood stairs to the first floor. I notice that Mena barely makes a sound, the only noise I hear is her soft, steady breaths, and I only hear those because she is barely an inch from me. Her footsteps are silent, her movements economical, and she seems to know to step just where I do to avoid the creaks in the stairs.

The first strike comes when we reach the top of the stairs leading into the kitchen. A wraith I've never met nearly takes my head off with a saw-blade machete. I duck back just in time, and the blade gets stuck in the molding of the doorframe. I take his head quietly with one of my Kukris and Mena catches his body as it drops, gently laying him down out of our way.

"This is a bad man," she whispers shuddering, and it takes me a moment to realize she is talking about his soul. I feel it, too. This is not someone who has been brainwashed or coerced into this. This is a man who would relish the kidnapping and torture of an innocent woman.

The hunger in me rises, the thirst to consume his soul. It's been too long since I feasted on the essence of an evil man, the fatigue in my body screaming at me to take it for myself. My mouth waters.

"Look away," I growl, not waiting to see if she complies as I grab the now-headless corpse, and my fangs lengthen and my jaw unhinges as I consume his soul, breathing it in, siphoning it from what's left of his body. Taking his blackness into me in a swirl of tar-like smoke, his body shrivels to a husk before disintegrating to dust in my fingers.

I look back, and Mena's eyes meet mine. I can tell she saw everything, even though I told her not to look. Her face gives away nothing, and real fear slams into me.

What if she is disgusted? What if she hates me?

"That was gross in an awesomely badass kind of way," she quips, and I breathe a sigh of relief. If I didn't need the strength, I wouldn't have done it in front of her.

"I needed the juice." I shrug, and she nods as we move on. We clear the kitchen, the dining room and have just entered the living room when the gunshots start, exploding a glass-bowled lamp right in front of me. Mena doesn't even flinch and pops off three rounds at the shooter on the stairs like she's playing a fucking video game. All three shots hit their mark: two hitting his chest and one hitting him right between the eyes, and he goes down instantly.

"They're wearing body armor. I can hear it," she murmurs distractedly. Her head cocks to the side as if she's listening to the house.

"There are more. I can't tell how many, but 'a lot' would be my guess," she whispers, and then hell starts. It's moments before we are pinned down behind the couch, caught between the freedom of the front door and certain oblivion by a veritable rain shower of bullets. I try to lay down cover fire, but I'm immediately clipped in the meat of my shoulder close to my neck.

"Fuck, fuck, *fuck,*" I mutter, grabbing at the wound, trying to staunch the flow of blood. I know I have to get us out of here before I can't travel anymore. I reach a bloody hand toward her when she scoots out of my grasp, staying under cover, but out of my reach.

"I need you to get out of this house, Asher," she orders me, eyes blazing gold as her Aegis flashes blue across her skin. Her voice has gone guttural, and I can tell by the curl of her fingers and the clench of her jaw, she has lost all ability to hold it in.

"Leave. Now. I'll come for you."

It kills me to have to leave, and as much as my protective instincts are screaming at me, I know she wouldn't do this if she had any other choice.

"Kiss me, Princess," I growl, and she does.

It's a kiss that says she's coming back to me, and it is the only reason I'm able to travel from that room, leaving her to take care of that hell on her own.

I make it to the truck but just barely. In my last seconds of consciousness, I see the house disintegrate in shards of blue light.

18

MENA

Seeing the red of Asher's blood in the darkness makes me lose a bit of myself. The part of me that cared but could still leave the people I love behind crumbles to dust in my chest. There is no way I will stand and let these vile men take him away from me. Take away the happiness I've been denied my whole life.

Ash's bloody hand reaches for me, and it takes everything in me to slide across the hardwood away from his fingers. I know what he's thinking. He wants to travel from the raining hail of bullets and get me to safety.

But I don't need saving.

He does.

"I need you to get out of this house, Asher," I tell him, and it kills me to do it. I want to keep him near me. Dress the wound. Make him safe. But I can't do that right now. I feel it rising: the heat, the flames, the energy. My Aegis is pricking along my flesh, begging to be set free.

"Leave. Now. I'll come for you," I growl, my voice a guttural order, one he has to follow. My life is tied to his now, and he has to do this for both of us. Black smoke coats his skin and then he slides away from me into the night. I wait for a few moments, letting him get as far away as possible before I loosen the reins and let my Aegis free.

I stand in the middle of the living room, letting the bullets pepper my shield. Nothing can get in, not unless I let it. I shrug off the katana, marginally upset that I didn't get to use it, and watch the wraiths, the men who stormed this house trying to steal my life, my mate, my happiness away from me. There are less than I thought. Only about ten or so. They stand on the upstairs landing, and on the steps of the staircase, lined up like a firing squad.

My light crawls up my bare feet, warming me, healing my aches, clearing my head. A smile stretches across my lips when it finally crests from my flesh and spills from my body. And I watch their surprised faces when they realize that they made the worst mistake.

With more power than I have ever felt surging from my skin, I let myself go free.

I wake up in a crater where Asher's living room used to be. If I keep blowing up houses, I'm going to run out of places to live real quick.

There is nothing left of the first and second floors, just smoldering timber of the ruined studs, broken and splintered, jutting up from what's left of the walls. The foundation is practically a bowl, the rubble raining all around me, burning to ash where it got too close to my shield. I feel the souls of the wraiths who have perished by my light, and each and every one of them was the worst kind of men. I feel no guilt for ending them. That might make me evil, too, but I don't care.

My only guilt is that I didn't leave Ash before I got too close. I shouldn't have let myself keep him. And now I can't let him go. I need to find Ash and get the hell out of here before the cops or the fire department or more wraiths come.

Tiptoeing through the rubble, I curse my lack of shoes as a piece of glass slices into my foot. I pluck the glass from my arch, blood welling instantly from the cut, but I keep going, making it to the driveway to see Ash slumped against the front passenger tire of the Jeep, eyes closed. His green flannel shirt is stained red, and my knees buckle a bit.

No. No, no, no, no, no, no.

Breaking into a run, I skid on the gravel as I come to a stop inches from him, my knees scraped raw in the slide. I barely feel it. My hands flutter for a moment, my brain blanking.

Blood. There is so much blood. Please don't let me lose him, too.

With shaking hands, I check his pulse and breathe my first sigh of relief at the fluttering beat—my ancient nursing skills finally being of some use. His heart is actually beating. Plus. But the rapid fluttering means he's going into shock—a definite tick in the minus column. I rip the sleeve from his shirt, yanking it off his good arm and wrapping it under his armpit and over the hole in his flesh. I pull it into a knot right over the wound, tightening it as much as I can, without ripping the fabric. It is a testament to how grave his injuries are that he doesn't make a sound, not even a moan of pain at the pressure of the dressing. I need a blanket to keep him warm, and he needs a healer. I can't take him to a hospital. I'm pretty sure they don't stock wraith type O.

Unbidden of my brain, I mutter expletives while I

work, searching the wheel wells of the Jeep for a spare key, hitting pay dirt on the third wheel I check.

Thank the freaking Fates.

There is no way I was going to be able to hotwire his Jeep. The last car I hotwired was a 1962 Chevy Impala under my father's intense scrutiny, and that was by the skin of my teeth.

You'd think I'd just be able to zap it started, right? Wrong. I have to tamp down every electrical impulse my body has just so I don't fry a car.

Okay. Breathe. Plan. What is the plan?

First up, getting him in the truck. Now, Ash is a big man, at least two hundred and thirty pounds, and I have to get him into this jacked-up truck without disturbing his shoulder or killing myself in the process.

Super.

I hit the "Unlock" button like I watched Ash do at the store and open the door. I search for the seat release and ratchet the seat back as far as it'll go. Jumping back down to the dirt, I have a mini logistics session in my brain, but quit when I realize I have to hurry. Ash is still losing blood, and I have no freaking clue what I'm supposed to do once I get him in the Jeep. Kneeling on the gravel, I grab his good arm and pull it over my back, easing most of his weight on my shoulders and back. It takes me five tries to stand up and eight tries to actually get him halfway into the seat. I curse my weak muscles as I push-shove him the rest of the way, making sure his feet are clear before slamming the shit out of his door, pissed at this whole situation.

Okay, step two: get him warm. I go to the back of the Jeep and search for a first-aid kit or a blanket or jacket or anything I can use. I find a thick fleece blanket, a first-aid kit, a gallon jug of water, a tool kit, and a jacket.

Grabbing the kit, blanket, water, and jacket, I then climb into the driver's side seat. I open the kit and see more crap than I know what to do with, and ninety-eight percent of it I have no idea how to use. I look for a cauterizing agent, but I'm out of luck. I zip the kit and fling it in the back, throw on the jacket, buckle him in, cover him with the blanket, and start chugging the water. It tastes musty, but I need to keep my wits about me and shock for me isn't an option right now.

On to step three, getting the hell out of here. Putting the key in the ignition, I pop the gear in "Neutral" and stomp the clutch, turning the engine over without stalling. Then, I thrust the truck in gear and promptly stall out. I start the engine again and pull out of the driveway, trying to remember the way back to the cabin in—what was that town called?

Grand Lake.

Okay.

Get back to Aurelia.

I can do this. I can remember the way. I can.

In the dead of night, there is no one on the roads, only the emergency response vehicles barreling past us once I finally make it to Highway 40. I shakily put the truck through the proper gears, trying to remember the other highway we turned off of when we hit Granby. I could try and use Ash's phone to call my sister, but honestly, I have no idea how to work it, whether or not I would fry it, or even if Aurelia would answer my call.

I hope they don't turn us away. I reach across the gearshift to check Ash's pulse. No better, no worse. I'll take it.

There weren't very many turns to get to Ash's house, and even though I studied the way as we went, I'm uneasy about my navigational skills. Papa told me to always know where I was, so I made sure I paid attention to road signs. I notice a black-and-white sign for Highway 34 and downshift with only minor sputtering to make the turn. Asher is going to kill me for hurting his tranny and probably his flywheel. I am awful at manual transmissions.

Only one more turn left, and that is the street for the house. I pass it twice before I finally get the right one, and once I get to the fortress-style wrought-iron gate, I know I'm in the right place. The seriously high-tech keypad has a "Call" button on it, and I gently press it about eight million times before someone answers.

"Do you have any fucking idea what time it is?" A rough voice squawks through the speaker, and my temper snaps.

"We were attacked, and Ash is hurt. Open the gate!" I scream into the speaker, and the buzzer sounds, the iron starting to move, much too slow for my liking. It takes every shred of willpower I possess to not ram the fucking thing. Once it's finally open, I haul ass up the long drive, screeching to a stop near the front door, parking be damned. The engine shudders to a stop, and I slam the emergency brake into place before hopping out onto the pavement.

I take a huge breath to scream for help, but I release it with a relieved sigh when I see Aidan, West and Cam smoking in the space just in front of me. Ian and Rhys burst from the front door, Ian carrying his notorious black medical bag.

"What happened?" Ian barks at me, and I tell him, leaving out the majority of the particulars, only telling him that Ash was shot in the shoulder.

"Get him to the dining room table," he orders, and the guys take him with them when they travel back to the house. Ian follows them, and I wobble, stumbling to my knees on the driveway when I try to take a step toward the door. I plop to my ass on the pavement, praying to everything I know in this universe that I can see those beautiful blue eyes again.

"Mena?" Rhys says as he kneels in front of me, but I don't see him, I'm still watching the door.

"Hmm?" I say, but I don't mean to. My brain is candy floss, and I am floating away. I feel the jacket jerk on my shoulder and hear my sister's voice rise with agony, but her voice sounds like it's in a tunnel.

"They're mated, Rhys. Her life is tied with his."

I don't get my wish. The last thing I see aren't Asher's winter blue eyes, but my sister's pale jade ones.

19

ASHER

WHEN I ROUSE FROM A DECIDEDLY RESTLESS SLEEP IN A BED that I know is not mine, in a room that is not in my house, and my mate nowhere to be found, pissed off is not even close to the emotion I'm feeling.

"Mena!" I thunder into the stillness of the room, worried and weak, my strength slowly coming back after healing such a lethal wound.

If I had gotten hit on the right side, it wouldn't have been too bad, but the left side—not so much. I'm kicking off the covers and about to stand when my beautiful mate comes walking in the door looking like she's been put through the wringer. She's still in the clothes she was wearing when the house was attacked, blood-soaked and soot-covered. Her hair is up in a haphazard ponytail.

Trailing her, is Ian and Aurelia. Her twin is on her like white on rice, riding her ass about something, when Mena explodes—figuratively, this time.

"Jesus fucking Christ, Aurelia!" she shouts as she whirls to face her sister. "I'll take a shower when I'm damn good and ready. If I wanted your opinion, I would ask for the motherfucker. Leave. Me. Alone. I want to check on my mate," she ends with a growl through gritted teeth.

Aurelia looks stunned for a moment before firing back, "You cuss too much." Her arms cross as if she's getting ready to deliver another lecture, but Ian cuts her off.

"Shut up, Half-Pint." Ian breaks in, shouldering Aurelia out of the way before Mena decides to tackle her and start the ass kicking she is dying to give. Mena uses Ian's distraction to come to me, standing in between my pajama-clad legs.

"Hello, my darling," she says as she cups my face and gives me a relieved kiss. Her knees buckle, and Mena's arms wind around my waist as her head hits my chest.

"How long have I been out?" I murmur against her hair, cupping the back of her head, massaging her scalp.

"Three days," she whispers, looking back up at my face, lips trembling as tears well in her eyes. She's breaking down, and by my guess, this is the first time in three days she's cried.

"Okay, you're up. Super. Asher, I'm glad you're alive. Can you get your mate to take a shower, eat something, and go to sleep?" Aurelia gripes from her position at the foot of the bed, eyes flashing in concerned anger. "Because she hasn't done any of that in the last three freaking days, and I'm ready to drug her ass."

The argument makes sense now, and I have trouble faulting her for it.

"And I keep telling you, I've gone months without any of that, and I survived just fine," Mena bites back, voice clogged with the emotions she's trying so desperately to tamp down.

"Great. Fabulous. You're a badass. You've proved it. Now, for God's sake, eat something, take a shower and. Go. To. Sleep!" Aurelia yells, throwing her arms up in exasperation.

"Princess," I murmur, my tone half-scolding and half-sorry. I did this to her, put her through hell.

"I blew up the house," she confesses and then she

breaks, chest heaving with sobs as she squeezes my middle. I haul her up, tuck her in the bed, and follow her in, propping myself up on the pillows so I can cradle her in my arms as she finally loses it.

When I look up, Ian is still standing there, brow creased, patiently waiting for Mena to either stop crying, quiet down, or it's entirely possible he's trying to figure out how big a dose of sedative she'll need.

Aurelia shoulders the door open, carrying a tray piled with food. Two huge bowls of chicken and dumplings, crusty French baguettes, and two bottles of water fill the tray, and by the determined twist to Aurelia's mouth, she'll force-feed Mena if she has to. Mena's sobs have quieted even though her tears keep flowing, and Aurelia plops the tray on her lap.

"Now, I made the bread and dumplings from scratch, so you're going to eat all of it."

"I thought you couldn't cook," Mena croaks from my chest.

"I said 'don't' not 'can't.' I hate cooking and kitchens in general, dishes most definitely, but I pull out the big guns for a crisis. You not eating is a fucking crisis. Eat," she says, brandishing the spoon like a weapon.

Mena reaches for the utensil, slipping it from Aurelia's fingers, and sits up, taking her bowl from the tray.

Before I know it, she's devouring the hearty soup like a frat boy with the munchies. She rips into one of the baguettes and dabs the rest of the bread in the soup, sopping up some of the broth before shoving the hunk in her mouth again.

I take my bowl, but before I tuck into my food, I ask, "How bad was it?"

"You or her?" Ian murmurs, eyeing Mena, and it occurs to me that she could have been hurt after I left, and I wouldn't have been able to do a thing to help her.

"Her first," I insist.

"Minor injuries. Cuts, bumps, and bruises mostly. My biggest worry was the shock, despite her efforts to keep it at bay. But she did good. Mena got you here, tried to take care of herself so she could do what she needed to, didn't wreck your Jeep, and didn't pass out until we got you inside. It would have been better if she called us, but given what she had to work with, she did good. Teach her how to use a cell phone, would ya?"

I can't believe I didn't take the time to teach her something so simple. "And me?"

"I need to check some things, but my guess is you're fully healed, which is markedly faster than expected, given your injuries. The shot was a through and through, but the bullet broke your clavicle and nicked your subclavian artery. Average bleed out for that is anywhere between two to twenty minutes and it's usually fatal. Now, I know I don't have to tell you that we do not regenerate at the same speed as phoenixes. You don't, and I sure as shit do not."

Ian pauses, trying to make a point, but I'm lost.

"He's attempting to tell you that mating me saved your life." Mena breaks in, talking around a hunk of bread. "I guess a mating shares the strongest traits between the spouses. So, congratulations, it's really hard to kill you now."

"Uh... what?" I sputter, almost choking on my food.

"You are organically drawing on my Aegis, so in life-threatening situations, I protect you," she garbles matter-of-factly around her food. "No spell, no pain, and apparently, you keep me from blowing shit up—your house excluded. Sorry about that one. I don't know if it's temporary or permanent, but I'm calling it a bonus."

"And you swear I'm not hurting you?" I ask as I turn to Mena.

"I promise, Ash," she assures me. "I wouldn't lie to you. Especially not about that."

Taking a deep breath, I try to wrap my mind around shared abilities between mates. I've never heard of a phoenix and a wraith mating in the first place, so I'm at a loss. Is this just because of Mena's Aegis or is this something else? Will she be harder for our enemies to find now that I've drawn from her?

Mena's spoon clatters in her bowl and she lets out a giant yawn.

"Okay, Princess, why don't you grab a shower, Ian can examine me, and then we can get some more rest? Sound like a plan?"

"Yeah," she says sleepily, slowly moving from the bed and padding sluggishly to the en suite bath. She doesn't take any clothes with her, and Aurelia rolls her eyes as she snatches Mena's bag from a leather armchair and trails after her.

"Did anyone ask John about it?" I ask, and I wish I hadn't. Ian's face falls, and I know it's bad.

"He's not doing so great, Ash," he says as he opens his med kit and takes out a stethoscope, fitting it in his ears before placing the cold metal over my heart. He listens in several locations and then switches to my back.

"Deep breath," he instructs, and I comply.

"Your heart sounds good, and your lungs are clear. I'm pretty sure you're completely healed. You don't even have a scar."

"How bad is he?" I murmur, ignoring my clean bill

of health, and Ian shrugs, swallowing hard as he grits his teeth.

"He's got maybe a week," he croaks, "and Voyt is coming here to talk about succession. Since he's the next male in the bloodline—however slight his claim to that bloodline might be. He wants to speak to John about handing over the reins early. He says there is a call for war with the phoenixes, and he's been recruiting. Evan is beside herself she's so pissed, and West can't calm her down."

Like he could if she decided she didn't want to be calm. Evan isn't one to just sit there and take some distant third cousin twice removed stealing her father's throne. Not to mention, we all know that if wraiths are behind Olivia's poisoning, Voyt is at the top of the list of suspects.

"Voyt—that fucking douchebag," I growl. "He makes Cam look like Mr. Congeniality. I haven't had a single conversation with that asshole that didn't make me want to punch him in his smarmy fucking face."

"West is going to bail, isn't he?" I ask, less like a question and more like a statement. I know how this is going to go. Bad.

"Probably. You know how he feels about being a leader," Ian grouses.

"It's bullshit, is what it is. He's been the only one

John has truly trusted. West knows everything. Every family, every transgression. He knows who to trust and who to kill. Hell, ninety-eight percent of the people who needed killing, West is the one who killed them."

"And that's the problem," Ian whispers, and it occurs to me that West might hate himself more than he hates the throne.

20

MENA

No one needs this right now. Not me. Not Ash. Certainly not John, and especially not Evan.

"This is such a waste of time," Aurelia grouses as she shrugs into a black suit jacket to cover the loaded shoulder holster under her right arm and spine holster at her back. "You know how this is going to go," she complains as she adjusts her black silk tank to cover a bit more of her generous bosom.

She fiddles with the jacket at the point of her shoulder and the pin-tucked ruffle at her back. Aurelia's long, black hair is pulled up off her neck and secured in a full topknot with several deadly-looking metal spikes, and her makeup is done up to full smoke, highlighting the paleness of her pupilless eyes and the sharpness of her cheekbones.

She moves to re-secure the throwing knives in her boot and then flips the wide leg of her black trousers over the holster. This is the third time she's checked her weapons, and if I didn't know better, I'd think she was nervous.

But I do know better.

She's not the least bit nervous—she's pissed. She'd rather go on an assassination mission than sit and play politics with someone she plans on killing, anyway.

"You know the last time I wore a suit around you, shit went awry," she grumbles to Evan. "This time will be no fucking different. Bad shit is coming, Evan. Bad, bad shit."

"And that is why I need you armed, but you need to look professional, and your weapons need to be concealed. You have to represent your people. I can't find Nicola, and headquarters has gone silent," Evan explains, and her voice has taken a lively quality that I haven't heard from her in the last week. "I can't find Kyle anywhere, and I haven't seen him since he left with her before the house was attacked. We are on the brink of a major shitstorm. I need to feel Voyt out. Dad needs to know what we're dealing with to buy us some time to defuse the situation. I can't just lop his head off and say 'nanny-nanny-foo-foo.' I need to be diplomatic—until diplomacy shits the bed and then I can make him die slowly."

She dusts imaginary lint from her dark wine-colored evening gown and adjusts the beaded sleeve. I admire the design of the dress: the bodice is a high crew neck, but mostly see-through mesh with slashes of beading that protects her modesty. One sleeve is the same fabric as her long flowing skirt, but the other is the mesh and beaded design of the bodice. What tips the sexy scale is the hip-height slit that exposes one shapely leg and one of the five-inch, suede, platform peep-toes adorning her dainty feet.

We abandoned the cabin in Grand Lake for the cliff-top house two days ago. In that time, I procured funeral clothing, an extra black tailored suit, and an evening dress that remarkably covers me from neck to wrists to toes and still makes me feel beautiful. Today, I get to wear the suit. Evan and Aurelia said these clothes were necessary for the coming meetings. Other than the one today, I'm unsure of what other meetings I'll need to attend and don't know why I even need to go to this one.

"And I have to be there because?" I ask for maybe the hundredth time in the last six hours. I don't think I need to be here. I have already helped as much as I am able.

After Ash awoke, I did what I needed to. After a full twenty-four hours of sleep, I gave some of my energy to Olivia and John. I didn't even need a spell—not that I couldn't cast one. I've heard the spell roughly a million times in the last fifty years. All I had to do was touch their hands, and their bodies hungrily pulled the excess from my bones without the agony of draining me dry. It felt organic, and I relished the use for my Aegis besides destruction. Olivia's eyes opened for the first time in a week and John's color came back. It won't sustain them, and I didn't cure them, but it will stave off death for a little while.

I just wish I could do more.

"We need you as a show of strength," Aurelia says as she adjusts the jacket of my suit. "You and I both know that it's likely that Voyt's men are the ones who attacked Asher's house."

While her suit has a bit more coverage so she can conceal her weapons, my jacket has a deep V-neckline, prominently displaying the lightning bolt Aegis marking on my neck. I think showing my mark would be like waving a red flag in front of a bull, but what do I know?

The suit also displays the relatively minor scarring

on my chest, but I don't mind it, mostly because of the nude beaded camisole I'm wearing underneath. I feel sexy in this outfit. My jacket is a slim cut with exposed velvet pockets on the front, and the ankle-length trousers showing off my height and the four-inch, thin-heeled, pointed-toe pumps.

"We want him to know you are alive, and you're strong, and you support us. You do support us, right?" Evan asks as she fidgets and then masks it by smoothing her already-meticulously coiffed hair, styled in a delicately messy chignon.

"You know I support you. You know Ash does, too. Don't ask dumb questions. You may not know me as well as my twin, but on the real stuff, our beliefs have always been the same."

Evan looks from me to Aurelia, and Aurelia nods in agreement.

"What she said. Quit being dumb. Okay, I'm ready. I'm going to find my mate, kiss him and see if there is any other prep we need to do," Aurelia says as she opens the bathroom door and flounces out.

Evan goes to follow her, but I gently clutch her elbow. I'm not shocking people anymore, and that scares me as much as it makes me smile. I worry I won't have enough in me to be an offensive weapon.

That I cannot protect them.

"A little red-haired birdie told me a very long time ago that you would be instrumental in taking Iva out. That you would be Queen. She told me I had to do whatever I could to help you. So that's what I'm doing."

Evan nods, raising her eyebrows and asks, "Nicola?"

"Yep. So if she can't be reached it's either because she has a reason, or they have done something to her. You will be Queen, she told me herself."

Evan inhales a deep breath, letting it out slowly. By sheer force of will, the tears pooling in her eyes don't fall.

"How are you doing?" I press.

"I've been better, but I'm standing, right? I'm doing better than my dad and a fuck-ton better than my mom. And I love a man who will not keep me. Even if marrying me—a woman he claims to love—means saving our race from that evil, twisted, murdering son of a bitch. So, I'm *super*," she says sarcastically with a half-shrug and a bitter smile.

"I have no advice to give you, Evan, but I can say this: you are a survivor. It may be the worst time in your life, but you will survive this. I promise. Even if I have to kill everyone in that room myself," I say waggling my eyebrows at the last bit.

Evan huffs out a laugh and gives me a wan smile.

"Let's go, Short Stuff." We link arms and head from

Evan's opulent bathroom through an equally sumptuous bedroom down a posh and regal hallway all the way to a sitting area filled with heavy furniture, crystal lamps, and priceless Ming vases. It is also filled with large men in very sharp suits. My eyes immediately move to Asher, and I release Evan to go to my mate.

Mate.

Who would have thought I could have this much, this quickly? Ash is everything I ever wanted for myself, and I need to keep him safe. To keep him safe, I need to present a front of a leader, even if that is the last thing I am.

"You look beautiful, Princess," Ash murmurs as he dips his head to kiss the tender spot right underneath my ear.

With my heels on, I'm eye to eye with him, and I love it. Running my hands over the arms of his suit jacket, I admire the way it clings to his broad shoulders and highlights his slim waist. I want to peel him out of it but refrain from doing so by a very thin margin.

"I love this suit. I'm going to have a grand time taking it off you later," he murmurs against my skin, inciting a shiver from me.

The ring of the doorbell sounds before I'm ready, and I feel a horrible chill steal its way down my spine. John steps into the room before the door opens for our guests and takes his place, sitting on a large, cream linen wingback chair. Evan positions herself on the seat at her father's right, Asher leaves me to stand behind John's chair, and Cam joins him. Aurelia and I take the love seat to John's left, with me sitting closest to Ash. Rhys stands behind Aurelia and West behind Evan, despite the irritated purse to her lips.

Ian moves to the shadows and Aidan answers the door.

Here we go.

Three men stalk into the sitting room behind Aidan, and I can tell already how this will unfold. One man is leading the trio of newcomers. His perfectly coiffed dark hair is swept back from his angular face. He has the features of a model, all sharp cheekbones and full lips, thick slashes of eyebrows highlighting pale eyes. He's tall, taller than Ash, and I dislike him on sight.

It's not just the horrible timing of his visit or the almost-forced politeness I notice on his face—it is the underlying expression, the one behind the fake remorse and false loyalty.

It's the hunger. Either for the throne or power—it's there.

The two men trailing behind him are both dark-haired and dark-eyed, looking similar enough in features that they could be brothers or close cousins.

They share the angle of their cheekbones and square of their jaws. Both dressed in dark suits, the one on the left is only marginally distinguished from his counterpart by the long hair pulled back from his face into a low ponytail.

Asher told me that news of John and Olivia's condition started filtering through the wraith community about a month ago. Just whispers at first, and that is how John knew there had to be either eyes in the house or on it. That's when they started to move, and he hid Olivia away in a house, even Asher had no idea of its location. Her guardians were left in the dark, sent to the far reaches of the earth to find a cure for their mistress.

After Javier had taken Aurelia, it was clear who the eyes belonged to but unclear how far his reach was.

John stands to greet Voyt, reaching to shake his guest's hand before retaking his seat. Voyt sits on the wingback opposite John, his minions standing at his back, mirroring Asher and Cam. Even though the room is tense, every person seems to be lounging on their seats or standing, idly waiting for this farce to begin.

"Voyt, I have some people I need to introduce you to before we begin our discussion of succession." He gestures to me first. "This is Mena Constantine, the last living full-blooded Aegis and rightful leader of the phoenixes." I let my Aegis free for a moment, waggling my sparking fingers at our guests. He then gestures to my sister. "And this is Aurelia Constantine, the last living seer, the only Aegis hybrid, and the woman who turned Iva to ash."

Then, John stands.

"And I'm sure you've met my mate," he says as Olivia strides into the room.

21

MENA

The click of Olivia's heels echo through the room. She's a small woman, not much taller than her daughter. Impeccably dressed in a blood-red chiffon evening gown, her stark-white, once-blonde hair pulled back from her face in a delicate twist. The dress is a Grecian, one-shoulder design with a fitted bodice and thigh-high slit. She's beautiful and elegant and regal, and I think I love her a little bit more—she has pulled off such a coup, without looking the least bit ruffled.

Glancing back at our guests, their expressions are not what I expected. I anticipated Voyt to be angry, to reveal a sign of distress that Olivia is not quite on her deathbed, but he's not. He seems pleased that his Queen appears to be on the mend.

His guardians, however, both look like they're ready to tear the room apart.

Interesting.

"Olivia, my Queen, I am so happy to see you," Voyt says as he stands, reaching for her hand and bringing his mouth to her fingers in a full bow. He rises from his position saying, "I am delighted to see that you are feeling better. When I received word that you were ill, I wanted to take a meeting to show my support and propose a few ideas to you and your mate."

No one in this room misses the fact he said "mate" instead of "King," or that he is deferring to Olivia instead of John. The insult may not be intended, but it's taken all the same. Voyt releases Olivia's hand and returns to his seat, and she takes the open spot on the love seat next to Evan.

"I am happy to see you as well, Voyt. How is your mother? I haven't spoken to Madeline in ages," she croons, her upturned midnight eyes turning soft.

Voyt's lips curve into a polite smile. "She is wonder-ful, ma'am. She speaks of you often."

"Oh, that is wonderful. We appreciate you taking the time to come to see us. Especially given the circumstances in the community," Olivia says, her voice and expression like butter wouldn't melt in her mouth.

"Yes, ma'am. It is a dark time. I wanted to discuss plans for the future. While I am technically the rightful male heir, I do not wish to step on anyone's toes." Voyt shifts in his seat. "I want to make sure a leader is chosen and appropriately trained, but now that I see you are both so healthy, I would rather talk about your intentions to settle the unrest in our community."

John reaches out and takes Evan's hand. "We do, in fact, have a plan to quell the unrest. Iva has been eliminated. Given her ability to control the phoenixes in her retinue, we believe the attacks on us were her doing alone. Their hierarchy is in tumult at the present, but Mena, here, should be the leader of the phoenixes. As she is now mated to a wraith, I am certain, once she takes her rightful position, Phoenix-Wraith relations should heal rather quickly. And as far as succession, I'm not sure if you've met my daughter, Evangeline."

"I have seen her in passing, but we have not been formally introduced," he says to John before addressing Evan, "And I am pleased to make your acquaintance, Evangeline."

His voice isn't quite a purr but almost, and his expression is hungry.

I realize that his hunger before wasn't necessarily for the throne or power, but maybe for the tiny blonde pixie. Voyt smiles earnestly at her, almost sheepish, the exchange earning him a menacing growl from West.

West looks three seconds away from losing his ever-loving mind, and his phase is almost immediate. His sharp talons rip into the upholstery of the couch, creating gaping gashes in the fabric.

If Voyt weren't already sitting, he would have taken a few steps back.

"Oh! My apologies. I had no idea you were mated," Voyt says, clearly abashed, and his face transforms immediately from hopeful to crestfallen.

"I'm not," Evan insists, glancing back at West with enough venom in her gaze to melt him on sight.

Something passes between them, and I realize that Voyt—if he's not a plotting, treasonous murderer—could be a viable option for Evan. West has not claimed her, has no plans to, and from what I'm guessing, this has been going on for a very long time.

Asher waited approximately two days to claim me. I could not imagine waiting for someone to deign to accept me. That would burn my soul so badly, I'm not sure I would recover.

"He is my guardian," she accuses, not taking her

eyes away from West, and his face seems to turn to stone.

Before the shutters fall, I glimpse the agony for a moment, and then it's gone.

"Evangeline is not mated," John cuts in, "nor does she have any plans to change that fact. As my only living heir, it was against the covenant for her to take the position of Queen without a mate—a rather archaic custom now that we are in the twenty-first century. However, I have written amendments to certain rules of the covenant, which have been approved by the Council. When I pass, she will be Queen. With or without a mate."

"While this is most irregular, I can see why you would choose that path," Voyt responds.

Since he seems one of the most diplomatic people I've ever met, I almost don't notice he did not give his opinion one way or the other regarding John's pronouncement. Instead, Voyt, who seems to be an expert at avoiding thorny topics, moves to continue the introductions.

"Please allow me to introduce my guardians, Segundo," Voyt points to ponytail guy, "and Guillermo," He gestures to the gentleman with shorter hair. "They are brothers to your Javier. They haven't spoken to him in weeks. Is he here? We would love to see him and Carver as well."

Unease falls over the room in a crushing wave. During my crash course in all things wraith, Asher explained what Revenants were. He also brought me up to speed on what happened in the weeks prior to my release. The attack on the cabin in Grand Lake, how Javier had likely been working for Iva the whole time.

How he attacked and nearly killed his mate. How he ate the hearts of some of the phoenixes who attacked. And how he stabbed and kidnapped Aurelia, bringing her like a present for Iva.

And these were his brothers.

John clears his throat. "Javier isn't here, Voyt. With Carver so injured, we had no idea that Javier had any living family. He did not speak of himself very often," John says, and he seems to be bracing himself for the next blow he has to deliver.

"Javier injured and kidnapped a woman in my care and tried to murder Carver. In fact, Carver is still healing from his wounds and has not regained consciousness. We discovered Javier was in league with Iva, divulging secrets. He also consumed the hearts of several combatants in battle. I hate to tell you this, but he had turned Revenant, and he was dispatched," John says, trying to gently break the news of Javier's passing to the two stone-faced men at Voyt's back.

The silence stretches thin for a long moment.

"Are... are you sure of this?" Voyt asks, seeming incredulous.

"Yes, I am afraid I am."

"Did you dispatch him?" Ponytail—err—Segundo asks, looking murderous.

John opens his mouth to answer, but he's interrupted by my big mouth of a sister.

"No, he did not. I did. I am also the woman he stabbed and delivered to Iva," Aurelia says, her voice even, her eyes unwavering.

She does not feel remorse, nor should she, but she also doesn't show weakness. I admire her and want to kick her right in her fool shin. Especially when Segundo and Guillermo exchange a look and go silent.

"I understand why you might be angry with me, but make no mistake, I do not relish killing, no matter how good at it I might be. My sister is mated to a wraith. My best friend is a wraith. I have been a part of the Black family for more years than I was ever a part of my own. They have sheltered me, protected me, and helped me for most of my life. Iva's assassination of so many is appalling, and it hurts my heart that so many wraiths have been lost. I am sorry for the loss of your brother, but he was working for Iva. He brought me to her to be tortured, and I will not apologize for saving my own life or the lives of those I prevented him from taking," she says, her voice calm and empathetic.

Segundo and Guillermo appear less than appeased, but they both nod all the same. I have a feeling we'll see them later. I'll be sure not to take any strolls in any dark alleys in the near future.

Voyt—to his credit—notices this and his face goes from surprised to what I can only describe as "damage-control mode."

"This news is... upsetting. I wish to postpone our discussion until my guardians can digest this information. Thank you for meeting with me. We will see ourselves out," he says hurriedly.

Voyt rises and walks to the door in a swift clip, and Aidan follows, showing him out. The room is tense for a few more moments before my sister breaks the silence.

"Well, that was less than helpful," Aurelia says.

"Oh, I don't know. Voyt is smarmy, but less of the antagonistic asshole you all made him out to be. And he has no clue that his guardians are piles of shit," I say, and Asher busts out laughing.

"It is so funny when you cuss, Princess," Ash says, chuckling.

"I agree. Both with the funny cussing and the

guardian's assessment. I still don't quite trust him, though," Olivia says, her smile broad and teasing, and I realize I have gained more approval from her. "You need to be careful, Ari-darling. I've heard stories of Segundo and Guillermo Cabal. They are not good men. I didn't realize Javier was related to those two jackals. I wish Carver had told us about his family. From what I knew, Javier did not speak to them after he took Carver as his mate. Silly prejudice, I know, but some people believe in the old ways. Those are the same people who will have issues with my Evangeline claiming the throne without a mate." Olivia cups Evan's cheek and looks into her eyes. "But we will change their minds, won't we, my love?"

"Yes, Mama," Evan croaks.

I get the distinct feeling in my gut that Olivia is telling her goodbye, giving one last piece of advice, one last message to her precious daughter. Olivia's face falls for a moment, but her smile returns, even if it trembles a bit.

I can feel it. My power was merely a Band-Aid for Olivia, and she has used it all up.

"I'm suddenly very tired. It has been an eventful and exhausting day," Olivia softly says, and then shakily stands to leave. Her color has gone from lively to gray in an instant.

"I'll go with you, Love," John murmurs and stands, taking her hand and gently wrapping it around his crooked arm.

They walk together out of the sitting room, and down the white, marble-floored hallway.

I feel it then, the overwhelming loss creeping into my soul, and I turn to look at my sister. Her eyes are glowing bright, tears dripping from her face, silent sobs choking her staggered breaths. Rhys kneels in front of her, holding her hands and coaxing her out of what is likely one of the worst things to see.

Olivia has been a mother to Aurelia—the only real mother she's ever had.

My tears come then, for the loss these people feel and what was denied my sister from our family. For Asher, for Cam, and Evan. For every life this delightful woman touched. For the loss these people feel, and my own. I barely met her, but there is no doubt Olivia was a wonderful woman, that I will never, ever get to know.

Asher's hands find me through the darkness of my tears, pulling me from the couch, wrapping me in a hug. We cling to each other in our shared grief.

Evan's gaze darts from her best friend to me, but she doesn't seem to understand that a phoenix can feel when a body is at its end. That we know when death is near, when a thread is drawn for cutting.

She had so much hope that I'd helped them, and this hits her like a sledgehammer. The dawning understanding on her face when she sees Aurelia crying...

She knows.

She doesn't wait to ask—she just smokes out of the room. When we hear her agonized wail a moment later, we know.

Olivia is gone.

22

ASHER

I have no idea what to do. I'm not sure anyone does.

I follow West on his quest to find Evan with Cam trailing reluctantly behind me. It wasn't far, just past the tree of life doors of the royal suite, but I hesitate before passing through them, trying to steel myself for what I know is just beyond.

But I know there is no real preparation for death. It comes as a surprise to us all, whether we want it to or not. When Mena's hand finds mine, I feel a small margin of relief before gathering the courage to walk into that room.

I wish I hadn't. I wish I could never see what will be burned into my brain for the rest of my life.

Evan is crying—no, crying isn't the right word. She is keening, great mutilated sobs filled with enough pain to burn us all. John has plopped on the chaise, Olivia draped, unmoving across his lap. Evan is kneeling at John's feet, clutching her mother's still hand. She's begging, pleading, promising everything in the world to get her to wake up.

This burns my soul with enough fire to consume me completely if I didn't need to stay alive for Mena. Mena's hand squeezes mine again, and she wraps those beautiful, strong arms around me because she knows.

Evan might be losing her blood, but John and Olivia are surrogate parents for every single person in this room. They took us in when we needed saving, or were cast out, or were unloved.

They saved us all.

Tugging Mena into my arms tighter, I rub my tear-stained face into her hair.

"Please, Mama. Please… don't leave me," Evan haltingly pleads, but Olivia doesn't answer her. That's when John reaches down, and rubs a thumb under Evan's eye, cupping her face with his free palm.

"Daddy. Please don't go. Please," Evan begs.

"Evangeline, my beautiful, strong, girl. We need to leave you now," he says, his voice barely above a whisper, thready with death breathing down his neck. "Stay strong. You can lead our people back into the light. You can do this, my dear. We love you, and we trust you. You are the best gift we have ever been given.”

When his hand falls from her face, Evan loses it. We all feel the loss as soon as his last breath leaves his lips, but Evan can't deal with the horrible agony bubbling up in her.

“No. No, no, no!” she screams, moving from one parent to the next, grabbing their faces to check for life.

She finds none. Evan can't hold in her phase anymore, and that's when all hell breaks loose. When Evan can't hold in her anger or fear or agony, things around her turn to dust. And this... this loss is the worst kind of hurt.

The floor beneath her feet abrades away, a swirl of dust and smoke surrounding her like a tornado. Her coal-black eyes turn vacant, and the floor and furniture near her begin to crumble.

West takes action, the only one of us brave enough to go toe-to-toe with Evan when she's lost it.

“Evan. Evangeline! You have to stop! You'll send them to Hell without meaning to. They don't deserve to go!” he screams in her face, latching onto her arm and shaking her hard enough to snap her neck.

She does a long, slow blink before her eyes regain their life, and then she rips her arm from his grasp and shoves him away with one small palm. No matter how tiny Evan is, she still made that one little shove count, because not only has West gone back at least five feet, the place on his shirt where her hand touched is now bare, bleeding skin.

The debris swirling around her slows, settling in a pile of dust at her feet.

"I release you," she whispers, and the occupants of the room, myself included, pull in a collective gasp.

"You may stay for the funeral, but afterward, you will leave this house. I *never* want to see your face again. If you ever truly cared for me at all, you will honor this," her command never rising above a murmur.

West hears every word, and he nods. Even when her eyes go dead, he still nods and leaves the room.

Mena tells me funerals are awful for everyone, and they are never really for the dead. "Funerals are for the living," she says.

I guess that's true, but I still hate them.

The preparation for the service has been exhausting over the last twenty-four hours, and Mena, Aurelia, Rhys, and myself have been handling the bulk of it.

Many families needed to be called, and since Olivia and John were actually good souls, security required a little amping up since phoenixes would be in attendance.

With the unrest, with so many wraith families slaughtered in the last few months, the likelihood that this could turn into a bloodbath is pretty high.

Evan asked both Aidan and Cam to be her new guardians. They accepted immediately, Cam faster than I thought he would, his tie to Olivia transferring to Evan now.

Wraiths from every corner of the earth have come, and as soon as the sun begins to set on this very long day, we can send Olivia and John to their rest.

So many have gathered in the gorge at the base of the cliff, where we can stay concealed from human eyes, and all be in one place at one time. A witch Aurelia knows offered to do a concealment spell for the event, but Mena nixed it, saying the magic could interfere with the passage of the souls.

She would know. Mena worked as a gentry for nearly a century before her capture, working with humans as either a nurse or a mortician, helping the neutral and good pass on.

Twenty-four straight hours of contacting families, making sure Evan was safe and ensuring that my mate and her family wouldn't be murdered, led us here, to the bottom of the gorge, in front of so many wraith families. They stand shoulder to shoulder, women in elegant evening dresses and men in suits, the river rushing around their legs, their gowns sweeping behind them in the water. The rest fill the shore, in the sand, on the rocks, filling the ravine to the brim.

Aurelia and Mena are in phoenix ceremonial funeral garb. Snow-white, one-shoulder, Grecian-style gowns, the fabric pools low on their backs, allowing enough clearance for their wings. Rhys, however, is not in anything that would be considered formal. Instead, he is dressed—like me—in full tactical assault gear. Black shirt under a bulletproof vest, black pants and boots, and every single weapon we can carry. Rhys' only concession in his vest is a missing back plate so his wings can burst free if needed.

We follow our wives, staying close, but assessing threats from the crowd. It also helps that Ian is at the top of the cliff concealing himself to the shadows with a sniper rifle.

One can't be too careful.

Aurelia and Mena phase at the same time, the twins igniting as one, blood-red and bright-blue wings rising in sync from their backs. Aurelia's are remarkably smaller than Mena's, and it takes me a minute to remember that the feathers of Aurelia's wings have been clipped.

I try to keep the horror off my face at the mutilation—something I have heard of, but never actually seen—and avert my eyes back to the crowd before looking at my mate again. Phasing is agony for Mena, but not a single peep falls from her lips. The twins move in unison to the bodies of the dead at the funeral pyre, Aurelia at John's side, and Mena at Olivia's. Evan smokes in at the head of the pyre with Aidan and Cam at her back and raises her hands to speak.

She asked me for help with the eulogy, but I directed her to Ian instead. Ian, while usually the joker, gives some of the best advice for someone so young.

"My mother gave me valuable advice over the years. She told me to never settle for a horrible haircut. She said if you could get away with wearing a higher heel, do it, but never be afraid of going barefoot." Evan chuckles before her voice breaks. "She said when I have my own ch-children, to give them twenty percent more hugs than they request and twice as many as I think they'll need. She also taught me how to be a strong woman. She taught me how to lead, how to be diplomatic, and instructed me when not to be. She is the voice in my head, my guiding star, and my conscience."

Evangeline pauses, gathering herself before she can continue.

"My father, in turn, taught me to be a strong leader. He taught me when to fight and when not to. He taught me how to think and how to breathe. He, along with my mother, will live in my heart for the rest of my days."

Evan nods and then bends to kiss the wrapped foreheads of her parents, tears wetting the white, gauzy fabric before she backs away. I do my best to turn off my emotions, but I feel a heaviness when I swallow, and when I see my mate barely holding herself together, the lump in my throat grows.

I allow myself one lone moment to grieve before swallowing it back. Evan signals to Aurelia and Mena, and they begin the funeral rites, murmuring the ancient language that guides the souls on. They then run their fingers over their charges' heads to their feet, igniting the silk wrappings and stacked wood of the pyre. The twins sweep their hands over the hearts of the dead, plucking glowing white ash from their still-flaming chests, take a deep breath and blow the ashes, scattering them to the beyond.

The whole of the assembly bows as one to Evan, and then all but five, travel from the gorge back to their homes. Wraiths do not believe in congregating after a funeral, they believe in solitude and reflection and mourning.

Of the five that stayed, three are known to me. Voyt, Segundo, and Guillermo.

Here we go.

The two I do not know—a man and woman—assess the threat of the seven of us from their positions in the water and travel hurriedly from the gorge.

Voyt approaches Evan, bowing low, seemingly oblivious to the turmoil behind him. His guardians do not mirror him, and the slight to Evan makes both Cam and Aidan growl through their fangs. Voyt rises and gazes back at his guardians, seeming confused and more than a little embarrassed.

"Did you know, Voyt, that my mother was being poisoned?" Evan begins, her head tilted to the side as if she's playing a stupid blonde when she is anything but. By his expression when he whips his head back to her, the answer is no.

"No. I did not. Olivia was beloved. I cannot imagine who would do something like that."

Evan rights the tilt to her head, leveling Voyt with a searing glare. "I can. Because I know who poisoned her," she snarls before she smokes out, traveling to the backs of Segundo and Guillermo.

Her tiny hands hit their backs between their

shoulder blades. Both men stand stock-still, eyes wide —frozen in pain.

"Oh, Voyt," Evan calls, and he spins, nearly slipping in the sand of the river.

"Your guardians had a hand in it, along with their brother, Javier."

"And who told you that?" Voyt sputters, his tone incredulous.

"I did," a deep male voice calls from behind Evan, and Carver walks slowly into the glow of the flames.

23

CARVER SAUNTERS TOWARD US AS MUCH AS HE'S ABLE. Dressed in a sharp black suit, he ambles slowly, his cane on the uneven ground making for slow going. A dark eye patch covers his right eye, barely visible underneath the heavy fall of his hair.

Ian said he was still healing from the injuries Javier slashed into his flesh, and it shows. Carver leans heavily on the wood and silver cane. The silver knobbed handle intricately carved into a lion's face, and the wooden shank a silky mahogany with a smooth ferrule.

"Javier was committed to his cause, I'll give you that. I mean, who else but a sociopath would fake being gay, stage a falling out with his family, and cut himself off from his friends just for a coup? A twenty-year-long coup. Commitment. Yeah, I'll give him that," Carver says bitterly, moving closer to this tense circle of frozen combatants.

"Like anyone should believe anything you say, *viado*," Segundo spits, but he remains unmoving, seemingly afraid of what will happen when Evangeline decides to flex her power.

"Yes, because being gay makes me a liar. So you're saying your brother wasn't a *viado*?" Carver asks tilting his head, the Portuguese slur flung back in Segundo's face.

Segundo grits his teeth saying nothing more.

"It really doesn't matter what you say or what lie you try to tell. I wouldn't believe you, anyway. Javier told me everything right before he attempted to rip my heart out and fucking eat it," Carver informs them.

"So my question, Voyt," Evan continues as if she were talking about her nail color and Carver hadn't just dropped the mother of all bombs, "is whether you were a part of it. Your face says no, but Javier had me fooled, so I'm not so sure."

"But I didn't! I didn't know. I was just going to talk to your mother about introducing us because you were unmated, and I saw you at an art gala in Denver months ago. I swear. Segundo and Guillermo have only been my guardians for less than a year," he pleads, hands raised in surrender.

"I'll take that into consideration, but the rumor was that you were recruiting for a war. What war were you planning to start now that Iva has been taken out, Voyt?"

At the accusation, Voyt straightens, his gaze turning sharp.

"I was not recruiting to start a war. I was sending aid to families and preparing for the eventuality of further attacks. That is not recruiting, that is being a competent leader. It is making sure our people are taken care of."

"So noted. I'll remember that while someone is trying to behead me in battle," she snarks. "You have no idea what it means to be a true leader. If you think shelling out more money to already-filthy-rich people who could just as easily provide for themselves makes you a leader, you are sorely mistaken. Since you've been so benevolent to our people, I'll let you live, but I want you to remember who your Queen is so you will watch as I turn your guardians to dust," Evan snarls, and then the screaming starts.

Javier's brothers do not die quickly. Their skin abrades away slowly, showing muscle and sinew and then bone, before the bone chips away to reveal their organs and blood. So much blood. Before that, too, withers away to dust. All the while, Evan watches as Voyt's face morphs from surprise to disgust to fear.

It's the fear she is going for.

After Evan is through with them, she delicately dusts off her hands, and walks to Voyt, grabbing him by the front of his shirt and raising him as high as her limited height allows, showing him that she is no wilting little flower.

"Mr. Voyt, I am letting you live so you can send a message to all your followers. My father made me Queen, and I will hold this position without a mate. Tell them what I do to traitors. What I did to the men who took my parents from me. If anyone tries to come and take my throne, I'll be sure to remind you of my message. Personally. After I kill every single person you hold dear. Have I made myself clear, Voyt?"

"Y-yes. You have, my Queen."

"Good. Oh, one more thing. Tell the leaders of each of the remaining head families that I will be meeting with them in one week's time. Tell them to be ready for my call," Evan murmurs and releases him so he *thumps* to the ground. Voyt wastes no time traveling from the gorge, leaving in a swath of smoke before he even regains his balance.

Then I feel it, the prickle of unease just as Aurelia screams, "Get down!"

We scatter: Cam and Aidan covering Evan, Rhys phasing on the fly and yanking Aurelia behind him, Carver wrenching a rapier from the head of his cane.

I try to move, to get in front of everyone so they can use the cover of my Aegis, but Ash bands an arm around my waist and hauls me to the slim cover of the brush line against the cliff face. I struggle against him, and his arm tightens before I feel his lips at my ear.

"Shh. We don't want to reveal your abilities just yet. These could be the same people who tried to get you in Fraser," he whispers in my ear, and I have to give it to him.

I didn't leave anyone alive in Fraser, so these guys wouldn't know the extent of my abilities. I can't just tip my hand now.

I need them closer, in a group, so I can fry them all at once.

Ash pulls me behind him, but I smack his arm and hold my hand out for a weapon. He rolls his eyes and brandishes a handgun from his left thigh holster, slapping it onto my palm as he raises his compact assault rifle and we both start firing back into the dark.

Then, I hear the sweetest sound, the thunder of the fifty-cal.

Thank the Fates.

It seems I praised the heavens too soon, though, because wraiths smoke in on all sides, advancing on us like a plague. But they aren't strategic, they are either untrained or disposable or both. I go for headshots, taking out five before my clip runs out.

Reaching for Ash, I rip the katana from its scabbard on his back, protecting his front as he drops his empty rifle and draws his kukri.

Aurelia and Rhys fight on my left as one, but Evan is having trouble with her guardians doing their job a little too well, refusing to let her fight at all. Carver ends up on my right, slashing two men down before lifting his apparently decorative eye patch and giving me a wink with his right eye before popping it back down.

He's not as injured as he pretended, and Carver spins and twirls with ease over the rocks and bracken, taking heads of three more men as he goes. The rest of the combatants left alive leave, realizing that they are being mowed down like grass, and then the firing from the cliff intensifies, and it's so much worse than before.

"Son of a bitch," Evan screams when she's grazed at the top of her arm, and Aurelia and I yell for Cam and Asher to get her the fuck out of here. They can't, though, because as soon as Cam touches her uninjured arm, she gives him a feral growl, and he rips his hand away as if burned.

Hell, he probably was.

Growling low in my throat, I catch Aurelia's attention as I notice three men and two women stalking toward us in the dim. They form a loose semi-circle, tightening the noose as they stalk closer. Other than the lit pyre and the Fireskin of Aurelia, Rhys and myself, there is no other light. I discreetly motion to the advancing group and give her a cutting signal. She nudges Rhys, and as one, we phase back, cutting off our light in the now-pitch-black gorge.

My vision is just fine in the shadows, so it's easy to stalk on my bare feet, closer to the rapidly advancing group of bastards, trying to kill my family.

And that's what they've become. This ragtag bunch of misfits are my people. Wraiths. Phoenixes. Doesn't matter. They are mine, and I will protect them.

I don't quite know what I'm capable of until it happens. My phase comes without thought and draws the fire of the five in the water and several from the opposite cliff top. I don't worry about the ones up high —their muzzle fire makes it easier for Ian to find them and take them out. The ones in the river, the ones dumb enough to get so close and not take the lead of their brethren, I make sure they pay. Their bullets ricochet off my shield, and bolts of lightning erupt from the tips of my fingers, snaking like ropes to wrap around their throats.

Their eyes bulge, but I don't hear screams.

Not that they'd be able to even if they tried.

The gunfire is gone, too. But I do smell cooked flesh and hear the muffled keening of their agony over the rush of the river. My power rises in me, tethering their bodies like a lash, raising them up from the water. The tips of their toes don't even touch the surface as I yank them higher and higher, their trousers and dresses dripping over the surface of the rushing water.

"Do you see? Do you see your friends? Do you see them burning?" I scream into the night, and then I take one long beat of my wings, rising from the riverbank, dragging them with me.

"Can you see them? Watch them die," I order into the dark, concentrating all my power into these would-be murderers.

I watch their bodies fill with blue light, their skin burning, cracking, failing to hold it in. Then they explode in a shower of ashes to the water and ground below. Beating my wings, I rise higher into the sky, making sure they hear me.

Making sure they can see what I am capable of. Making sure they know.

"They burned for their crimes. They burned for their defiance of your Queen. If any of you come after me or my family again, I'll do the same to you," I growl into the stillness.

Silence is my only answer.

EPILOGUE

MENA—ONE MONTH LATER

I ROLL OVER IN THE WARMTH OF THE BED AND FEEL COLD sheets where my mate should be. Slowly opening one lone eyelid, I'm irritated until I smell the coffee. The other eyelid finally decides it's okay to open. Asher is sitting shirtless, just in his gray pajama bottoms, in his new reading chair, bare feet crossed on the ottoman I made him get.

"Got any of that for me?" I croak, sleep clogging my throat.

"Me, the book, or the coffee?" he asks, his eyebrow raised, not looking away from the page until he can blindly locate the bookmark on his left armrest.

"The coffee. Duh," I quip as I roll mostly naked from

the bed and pad over the hardwood to sit in his lap. I kiss him on the lips before reaching across him and bring the sweet nectar of life to my lips, the large diamond of my four-carat, cushion-cut, pink diamond wedding ring winking at me in the morning light.

"Well, at least you paid the toll," he murmurs against the sensitive skin of my neck, and the beginnings of an exquisite make-out session that will most definitely lead to more sex is interrupted by the doorbell.

Grumbling, Asher presses one last kiss against my lips before setting me off his lap and padding out of the room to answer the door of our new house on the outskirts of Denver. It serves as a phoenix headquarters of sorts with the new wraith hub just forty-five minutes away in a high-rise downtown. It has been a month, and since Nicola still hasn't resurfaced, Aurelia and I took the mantle as leaders.

We have had feelers out almost everywhere looking for her, but when an Oracle doesn't want to be found, she doesn't get found.

I refused to set a single foot in Iva's house in Oregon. Aurelia said since we'd both been tortured there, setting the motherfucker on fire was a viable option. We didn't, but it was tempting.

We're still working out the kinks, mostly with the

Oracles, but it is getting better. Or it would if I could get Aurelia's head out of the toilet.

For a woman who claims to be psychic, she sure doesn't realize when she's pregnant very quickly. Rhys and I are still trying to persuade her to take a test, but she's stubborn. She can be stubborn all she wants—I'll get Ian to take blood on her tomorrow.

We'll just see who combat trains while pregnant.

Throwing on a bra, a tank, a fuzzy grandpa sweater, and a pair of jeans, I pop in the bathroom to tame the sex hair and brush my teeth before heading for the stairs.

"Mena!" Asher yells for me as I hit the landing.

The alarm in his voice has me running for my mate before I can blink.

Asher kneels next to a large man lying on the cold tiles of the foyer. He's bloody and dirty and enormous. He lays there nearly naked, only wearing tattered jeans, no shoes or shirt at the start of a Colorado winter. His hair and beard are wild and dirty, as if he's been inside the walls of a cell for a while.

The part that concerns me is, he keeps repeating a name—the name of a woman I owe my life to. The woman we've been searching for.

"Nicola... They took her from me. They took her over... They put Iva in her. They took her over... Nicola..."

he rasps before he loses consciousness right there on the cold tile floor. I look up to Ash, but he's already answering my question.

"This is Kyle, Nicola's mate."

Son of a bitch.

Thank you so much for reading Death Kissed. Mena & Asher have a very special place in my heart. But we aren't quite done yet! Next up is Evan & West and all the heart wrenching, rejected mates chaos that is to come.

Fate Kissed is next on the menu, and I hope you're buckled in to see the heartbroken, newly crowned Wraith queen and her swoony, over-protective mate.

Grab Fate Kissed today!

However, if you would love to see a glimpse of the couple that started it all, you should turn the page to access this epic holiday bonus scene. I hope you enjoy it!

Want the skinny on future releases without having to follow me absolutely everywhere on social media?

Text "LEGION" to (844) 311-5791

BONUS SCENE

Dear Reader,

I hope you enjoyed Death Kissed. Mena & Asher have a very special place in my heart, and I am absolutely ecstatic for you to read them. But the couple that started it all needed a teeny bit of attention...

I have a holiday bonus scene for you as a thank you for reading. All you have to do is click the link below, sign up for my newsletter, and you'll get an email giving you access!

https://geni.us/dk-holidaybonus

Living up to the family name is going to get me killed.

As the newly crowned Wraith Queen, I have some big shoes to fill. Especially while mending a broken heart.

But the mess left in the wake of my parent's death won't get cleaned up by itself, and the enemy who murdered them has taken the man I love.

**_I'll show them exactly what their new Queen is
capable of._**

EVAN

I'm livid. This isn't a new thing for me. Lately, I get
angry at the drop of a hat. It's no surprise, I mean come
on. Who wouldn't be mad? I'd figure today of all days I
would get to just be sad.

I put my parents to rest today. I should be crying
into a big glass of bourbon right about now.

Nope, not me.

Instead, on the first day of my rule, I not only had to
fight for my life, but I also had to _fight to fight_ for my life.
I was treated like a child by the very men I'm supposed
to lead. Sure, I killed the men who conspired to murder
my parents in probably the worst way I can think of, but
in the grand scheme, I didn't get the head of the snake. I
don't even know who the snake _is_.

That will have to come later.

And then I have Idiot One and Idiot Two trying to
keep me from fighting alongside my family.

I don't think so.

I take a look around at the aftermath of the gorge.
Other than some scorched rock, one would never know

so many lost their lives here. In the silence, now that the guns have spent their rounds and the weapons have all been sheathed, the only sound apart from the rush of the water over the rock is the faint beat of Mena's wings as she searches for another threat.

She won't find one.

Wraiths rarely fight if they think they can't win. This is why we've lived in 'peace' for so many years. Why start a war when you can just kill someone in the dead of night and blame somebody else?

Wraith logic. We are a sunny bunch, aren't we?

Mena circles once, twice, and then finally lands on a large boulder jutting into the water from the shore. Phasing almost immediately, she jumps from the rock into Asher's arms, and a new ache wrenches in my chest. *West.*

He didn't come, didn't stay. He didn't help.

The ragged edges of my heart start bleeding once again. I know I released him. I know I told him I never wanted to see him again, and it's true—I don't. Not really, despite the pitiful whining of my heart. I couldn't keep relying on someone who was never going to choose me—who was never going to stay with me.

I can barely wrap my mind around the fact that he *knew* we were mates, knew that the Fates chose us to be together. He felt it with me and decided to deny me. For one hundred and nine years he's denied me. Turning his nose up at all we could be.

You'd think I'd know better by now.

I finally wised up, but only a little, because I was still shocked when he didn't come to the funeral. *Shocked.* How stupid can I be?

A lot, apparently, because I'm still stinging with jealousy from watching Mena and Asher, and as each beat of my heart begins to ache in my chest, I realize I just can't take one more thing today. Before I can leave, my best friend in the entire universe grabs my hand. I'm not looking at her, but I know it's Aurelia. The pain in my chest eases for a moment, and I have never been more glad she is here with me.

Saving me from the fire from the very first day we met, Aurelia knows me better than anyone—even if I've been keeping huge secrets from her.

Pulling me close, she wraps her arms around me, the natural heat of her skin warming me.

"I'll only be able to stall them for a few minutes so you can get your shit together, but *only* a few minutes. The house is empty, so use your time wisely," she whispers into my ear before giving me another squeeze.

I can work with a few minutes. That is just enough

time to sling back a shot of bourbon and get out of this stupid gown. Who decided to make funerals formal attire only, for pity's sake?

Not taking the time to ponder the origins of Wraith customs, I travel from the multicolored rock floor of the gorge to my room in the cliff house.

It is an opulent room—far too rich for my taste—but Mama decorated it for me, and I didn't have the heart to tell her it wasn't me. Now, that she's gone, I can't imagine changing it.

The walls are papered in a lightly textured, luminescent cream. In fact, most of the room is in shades of white and silver from the wallpaper to the mirrored side tables. The only color—and my only contribution to the design of the room—is from a plush magenta area rug that is begging me to walk on it. I detour around the white leather sitting chairs just so I can walk across the soft shag on my way to the liquor nook hidden away by an antique-white paneled cabinet.

My mother and the white. *I'm not a virgin, Mama. That ship sailed a long time ago.*

I pull a squat tumbler from the lowest shelf and splash a healthy measure in the glass. I only get a single swallow in before Cam and Aidan bust my door open like an episode of Cops. They file in my room like they are my wardens, and I realize now, letting them get away with the shit they pulled in the gorge was a mistake on my part.

"Well, that was unnecessary," I say before I can stop myself, and I'm happy it comes out calm as you please instead of the seething rage bubbling in my chest.

"What the hell do you think you're doing, Evangeline?" Cam thunders, his hulking form fills the doorway, the black of his clothes making him look only more ominous.

He is chastising me like a naughty toddler.

Yep, big mistake on my part. *Sorry, Papa, I've failed you already.*

Taking another swallow of my bourbon, I carelessly fling the glass back in the cabinet. Before the tumbler can stop spinning on the bar top, I've traveled to the pair of them and have Cam face first on the tile with his hand pinned behind his back.

First my parents, then West, now this. I am already shitting the bed at this whole leader thing. I am done failing, and if there is anything I learned from my father, it was sometimes lessons need to be taught the hard way.

As my talons gouge into Cam's face, I turn my black eyes to Aidan, and by his expression, I can tell he didn't expect me to know how to fight nor did he know I could take someone much bigger than myself down.

We've fought together. He should know better.

"I assume this tantrum is because I left the gorge?" I ask, and Aidan hesitantly nods.

Cam doesn't move an inch, and I don't blame him. One wrong move and his eye is going bye-bye.

"I have some issues with your behavior at the funeral. First and foremost, you held me back from fighting," I say calmly.

"We did our job. We were keeping you safe," Aidan gently pleads and while I appreciate the sentiment, I can't abide by it.

"Would you have refused to let my father fight? Would you have tried to take that away from him?" I ask, and I can tell my question hits home.

He has undermined me without meaning to, and at the realization, Aidan's face goes white.

Aidan and Cam have been with my family long before I was born. They see me as a child, a little sister, and while I trust them with my life, I can't trust them to guard me against the dangers of this reign for another second without this lesson.

"No. You wouldn't," I scold, answering for him.

"But you..." Cam begins.

"Do. Not. Presume to tell me what I can and cannot do. I am your Queen, your leader, and you will treat me as such or I will make you regret it." I say through gritted teeth, and while I feel slightly guilty for smashing his face on the hardwood floor, it has to be done.

I love Cam, he is the big brother I never had. He has tended to more scraped knees than any grown man should, but family or not, he cannot keep playing big brother.

It will get us both killed.

"I love you both, but I will release you and get someone else if you can't get it through your thick skulls that I'm not a delicate little flower. I know how to handle myself. And if you undermine me again, I will make your release the permanent kind. Do you understand me?" I question as I retract my talons from his face and travel to my feet.

I get a reluctant nod from Cam as blood wells from the cuts in his cheek. Cam and Aidan both take a knee of supplication, and when they rise, five little ribbons of red have made their way down Cam's face.

"Good. If it makes you any feel better, I will continue my sparring sessions with Aurelia to keep my skills sharp. She's been training me for a decade already, I see no reason to change things up now," I admit to a stunned Aidan.

"West let you..." Aidan says, and his eyes widen as he trails off realizing his mistake.

Just the sound of his name slices into my chest, and I steady myself against the blow.

"West was not aware. He was my Guardian, not my father. I don't want to hear his name again. Now, no offense guys, but I need some alone time. I'm going to go drown my sorrows in some bourbon and take a bath. I want the door fixed before I get out. Oh, and if you bust in my room again, I'll cut something off of that you need. Understood?" I ask, but it isn't really a question.

They both got a freebie pass for pulling that bullshit in the gorge. I can't be that lenient again.

Walking back to the cabinet, I snag the bourbon and my glass from the bar top and head to the en suite bathroom, gently closing the door when I want to slam it. Flipping on the taps before moving to the walk-in, I pull the zipper down on my dress and slip it from my shoulders. Carefully putting it on the thick, wooden hanger, my mind finally catches up with me. Black gauzy fabric, heavy, black beading, I hate this dress. I want to burn it. I want to rip it to shreds. This is the last thing I wore when I saw my parents for the final time.

It's tainted, infected with the bitter loss I'm trying

so hard to stomp down into nothing. It's then that I let myself break a little and hug the now-cold dress to me as I crumple to the plush carpet.

I allow myself three minutes. Just three to vent some of this agony. I have to let it out now—where no one can see. I can't be weak, can't break.

Stemming the flow of the pain leaking from me, I climb to my feet and hang the dress on the rung. I can't let it go now. It was the last thing my mother picked out for me, the last thing we ever shopped for. Had I known at the time it was going to be my funeral dress, I wouldn't have ever bought it.

I reach up and straighten the strap on the hanger before running my fingers down the bodice.

Miss you, Mama.

I suck in a huge breath and let it out in a gust, shoring up my walls again and turn from the closet to turn the taps of the large clawfoot tub off. Filling the tumbler to the brim, I set it in the fancy teak bath tray spanning the width of the tub, and before I can think better of it, I plop the bottle of bourbon right next to it.

One night to grieve.

I need this time to deal with losing my parents. Time to put on my big girl panties and rule as good or better than my father did. My father had to worry about his mate, and that guided his decisions. Some of those, I hate to say, treaded the safe path rather than the right one. He stayed safe to keep his mate alive.

I don't have one of those, and I probably never will.

Nope.

Safe is not for me.

I'll do the right thing instead.

Grab Fate Kissed today!

BOOKS BY ANNIE ANDERSON

SEVERED FLAMES

Ruined Wings

IMMORTAL VICES & VIRTUES

HER MONSTROUS MATES

Bury Me

SHADOW SHIFTER BONDS

Shadow Me

THE ARCANE SOULS WORLD

GRAVE TALKER SERIES

Dead to Me

Dead & Gone

Dead Calm

Dead Shift

Dead Ahead

Dead Wrong

Dead & Buried

Soul Reader Series

Night Watch

Death Watch

Grave Watch

The Wrong Witch Series

Spells & Slip-ups

Magic & Mayhem

Errors & Exorcisms

The Lost Witch Series

Curses & Chaos

Hexes & Hijinx

THE ETHEREAL WORLD

Phoenix Rising Series

(Formerly the Ashes to Ashes Series)

Flame Kissed

Death Kissed

Fate Kissed

Shade Kissed

Sight Kissed

ROGUE ETHEREAL SERIES

Woman of Blood & Bone

Daughter of Souls & Silence

Lady of Madness & Moonlight

Sister of Embers & Echoes

Priestess of Storms & Stone

Queen of Fate & Fire

To stay up to date on all things Annie Anderson, get exclusive access to ARCs and giveaways, and be a member of a fun, positive, drama-free space, join The Legion!

facebook.com/groups/ThePhoenixLegion

ABOUT THE AUTHOR

Annie Anderson is the author of the international best-selling Rogue Ethereal series. A United States Air Force veteran, Annie pens fast-paced Urban Fantasy novels filled with strong, snarky heroines and a boatload of magic. When she takes a break from writing, she can be found binge-watching The Magicians, flirting with her husband, wrangling children, or bribing her cantankerous dogs to go on a walk.

To find out more about Annie and her books, visit www.annieande.com